The Season That Was

This book has been independently published by S & SP Publishers.
All books, both paperback and Kindle versions, are available by
visiting amazon.co.uk

Also independently published by S & SP Publishers:

Available in paperback

The (Not Quite) Complete Works of…	Stephen E Pennykid
Arnold and Beyond – The Good Old Days	Nancy Meller
Bones to Stones and Beyond	Martin Litherland
Richard III – Death and Resurrection	Martin Litherland

Available on Kindle

MisHits of the Sixties	Stephen E Pennykid
MisHits of the Sixties Volume 2	Stephen E Pennykid
American Artists	
MisHits of the Sixties Volume 3	Stephen E Pennykid
The 'B' Sides	
MisHits of the Sixties Volume 4	Stephen E Pennykid
Instrumentals	
Chief Inspector Robert Casey Short Stories:	Stephen E Pennykid
The Blackberry Way Murder	
Tragedy	
The Sound of Silence	
Communication Breakdown	Stephen E Pennykid
This Boy	
Smoke Gets In Your Eyes	
The News From Spain	
2 Spooky	Stephen E Pennykid
The Sins of Others	
A Trip in Time	
Look at my Bones – Poems of Richard III	Martin Litherland
Poems of the Lost World	Martin Litherland
Inca Treasure	Martin Litherland
Romantic Rocks	Martin Litherland
My Name is Eve; Black is my Face	Martin Litherland
Early Memories	Martin Litherland
The Moment Trilogy	Martin Litherland
The Season That Was	John Meller

Children's Stories on Kindle

Two Tiny Christmas Wishes	Eddie Penny
Yesterday's Train – An Olympic Record	Eddie Penny
Christmas Wishes	Santa Rowly

The Season That Was

JOHN MELLER

S & P Publishing

CONTENTS

PROLOGUE

It was a typical evening in the Smith household. Steve was sprawled out on the lounge sofa, half watching Liverpool trample all over some typical godforsaken tinpot waste of time foreign outfit. Whilst doing so he was flicking absent-mindedly through the local pathetic attempt at an evening newspaper. It was Whingeing Wendy's turn to cook, so Steve's Beloved was in the kitchen, preparing some strange, no doubt inedible, fish pasta concoction. As the football commentary was only at volume level nine, Steve could just overhear the smaller kitchen TV. The fourteen-inch colour portable was bellowing out the latest 30-minute episode of the UK's second most popular soap opera. Despite such ear-shattering distractions, Steve had already knocked back a couple of cans, and was by now beginning to gently doze off.

The phone rang.

'Stuff it,' said Steve, waking abruptly from his stupor. 'Who the hell is that?' He dragged his grey haired, fourteen stone frame out of its previously more than comfortable position, and sulked dejectedly across the litter strewn carpet towards the offending piece of 1930's Bakelite. He picked up the receiver. And dropped it. It fell heavily against the recently purchased limed oak cabinet. Franticly unravelling the overly twisted cable, he recaptured the elusive mouthpiece and spoke aggressively into the most annoying contraption that the world had ever invented. Alexander Graham Stupid Bell had a lot to answer for, in Steve Smith's eyes. Especially at this time in the evening.

'Hello. Perfect Plumbing speaking. What do you want?' he announced brusquely, to the invasive nosey busybody who'd had the gall to spoil his quality time. If it wasn't a plumbing client moaning about the quality of his work, it was bound to be some stupid plonker trying to sell him double glazing. Otherwise it would be yet another boring invitation to a three-day seminar on the pros and cons of 19mm diameter plastic tap washers.

The reply came from a posh male voice.

'Hello, Mr Smith. My name is Ted Carruthers. You don't know me, but I'm from the Evening Gazette.'

Steve Smith woke up. And moved rapidly into defence mode. He replied. 'I didn't do it. I'm denying everything. I'm phoning my solicitor..........'

The caller butted in. 'Don't panic. I'm not interested in your misdemeanours. It's nothing to do with that. We're thinking of running a weekly piece on old local sports teams, and I've been flicking through some of our editions from 25 years ago. We've stuck the names into a hat and Barmfield Cricket Club has come out as our first choice. We know that they are no longer in existence, but we've found your name from the Association. I wondered if you'd like to call in for a chat, sometime?'

'Yes. Er, yes. Of course. Er...'

'Good. Don't worry at the moment. I can hear that you're watching the footie. I'll phone you back in the morning. As I said, my name is Ted Carruthers. Speak to you tomorrow. Cheers.'

Steve frantically tried to move his brain out of reverse. Grinding slowly through neutral, it eventually reached first. 'What was that all about? Why had the newspaper rung him? There were twenty or so guys who played for Barmfield around the same time that he had done. Why choose Steve Smith out of that lot? In fact why choose Barmfield Cricket Club at all?'

Steve covered the most recent scratch in the cabinet top, by carefully moving the local Yellow Pages over it. He then drifted through to the kitchen. Luckily, Whingeing Wendy hadn't yet noticed his arrival, so he could confidently secrete another can from the fridge. The supersonic boom-like noise created by Corodale Enders told him that his wife was not aware that BT had, yet again, deliberately spoilt her husband's evening. It was clear that his petite, mousy haired partner of the last twenty odd years was currently more interested in amorous flings between barmaids and brickies. Likely as not she would still have been ensconced in the ruddy thing, even if her spouse had, at that moment, announced that the house was burning down. Or that the Earth was about to hit the Sun. Steve the Perfect Plumber traipsed forlornly back to the lounge, sat down yet again, and poured himself his third pint.

An hour or so later, Mr Stephen Smith informed Mrs Wendy Smith about the telephone conversation. Her initial reactions followed a well-trodden path. Was her husband deliberately winding her up? Had he supped ten lagers instead of the usual four? Or were her earlier suspicions correct, in that senile dementia had finally kicked in? She followed her standard practice of doubting her husband at every available opportunity. Firstly she checked the 1471 number, in an attempt to verify that there had been an incoming call in the first place. Noting loudly, as she did so, that the mouthpiece end of the valuable antique had recently developed a small crack. And also that the Yellow Pages had been moved two and a quarter inches to the northwest of its standard position. Having concluded this detailed checking process, it still took several more minutes for Mrs Wendy Smith to fully convince herself that her hare-brained husband was unusually sane and relatively sober.

'Well, Steve,' pronounced Mrs Doubting Thomas. 'I'll be fascinated to hear about what that newspaper bloke says in the morning. Assuming that he does actually phone you again, of course. Which is unlikely, knowing you as I do. You seem to have made a career out of upsetting everyone that you talk to. By the way, when are you going to spend an evening not lying on the sofa? There are lots of jobs that need doing, you know. You get lazier by the day. You'll weigh twenty stones soon. I'm going back to watch the kitchen television. It's your turn to wash the pots. And, despite your usual negative comments to the contrary, I personally really enjoyed the trout and tomato tagliatelle, cooked with parmesan en-croute. I got the recipe from that cookery book that your Mum bought us when we got married'.

Steve took the next morning off from his Perfect Plumbing business. Whingeing Wendy, being a Department Head at a local Secondary School, was not allowed such luxuries.

It was 9.37am when Ted Carruthers called back. By 11.28am, Steve Smith was sitting outside a very plush glass office door. And by 11.32am, it opened.

A large pinstripe suited businessman stood there, filling the doorframe and almost completely blocking out the light. He was perhaps in his fifties, a similar age to Steve. He looked very much the business tycoon, with slightly greying brown hair, and a thick brown moustache. He reminded the visitor of one of those Russian politicians of the fifties.

'Please come in, Mr Smith,' said The Giant, in his public school accent. Your Local Friendly Number One Heating and Ventilating Specialist duly obliged. He entered a very plush office, and sat down in a very plush leather chair.

'Thanks for turning up, Mr Smith. Sorry that you've had to take the morning off work. I appreciate that you're a busy, hardworking chap. Coffee's on its way. I'll get straight to the point. I'm the Deputy Editor. We want to do a regular story about a local sports club. Ideally a club from the past, with a bit of history attached to it. The item will go out on Tuesdays. We think that we can run it for perhaps fifteen to twenty weeks before the readers get bored to tears with it. Ideally we'd like to be printing sooner rather than later, but we don't really want to start on Week 1, until we've got all the rest of the story more or less completely finished and ready to roll. That would be too big a risk, especially if someone like you is doing it. We've got ghost writers and checkers who can help out when we get nearer to the final thing, but we need an ex-Club player or official to prepare the basics. The way we see it, if someone close to the Club can do the donkeywork, we can then tart it up a bit where necessary. What do you think, Mr Smith? Or shall I call you Steve?'

Mr Pinstripe's visitor had by now developed a yet more furrowed brow. He replied thoughtfully to the host. 'Yes, you can call me Steve. That's fine. But I've got so many questions to ask. I don't know where to start. And I have got a business to run, you know. I can't spend all day every day working for you. I was very busy last night when you phoned; I was working on my books.'

Recalling being deafened by the previous evening's European tie blaring out down the phone line, and by the semi-slurred voice of the call's recipient, Deputy Editor Ted Carruthers smiled knowingly.

'Sorry, Steve, I didn't realise that you were working again

last night. It must be a hard life running your own business. You ought to try to get a few minutes break, now and then. All work and no play does a man no good. I'd recommend an occasional restful evening. Perhaps a few pints in front of the TV. Rest works wonders, you know. Anyway, fire away with your questions, Steve.'

'Well, in no particular order, my initial thoughts are as follows. Firstly, why do a story at all? Secondly, why pick Barmfield Cricket Club? Thirdly, how did you find my name? Fourthly, what makes you assume that I'm capable of doing it? Fifthly, ...'

'Stop,' said the Lookalike Russian Politician. 'Don't say anything else for a minute. For Christ's sake. I'll try to fill you in a bit more first. We believe that our readers will be interested in a sports club story; particularly a cricket based one. We've done market research on it. As I said last night, Barmfield were picked at random. But our starting list only comprised about fifty or so of the better-known local sports clubs from the recent past, out of the five thousand or so that there are altogether. So Barmfield's chances of being selected were one in fifty, rather than one in a lot more. In order to choose the particular club, we wrote each of the fifty or so names on a separate little piece of paper, and I then put all the names in a hat. The Office Cleaner was then invited in, and asked to pick one of the bits of paper out of the hat. She was told that she could pick whichever one she wanted, as long as she closed her eyes whilst she did it. And she happened to select the piece with Barmfield CC written on it. Out of interest, we then tipped the rest out onto the floor and allowed her to open her eyes before she hoovered up the mess.'

Proud of such technically-adept ingenuity, Ted Carruthers grinned at the visitor, awaiting a complimentary response.

But he didn't get one. Steve Smith just nodded, attempting to appear intelligent and vaguely interested. His mind was working along the lines that there could be a day's expenses in this, if he dragged things out a bit longer. Before he then told Mr Stupid Pinstripe to get stuffed, of course.

The newspaperman carried on. 'We made sure that we'd got at least one definite contact name for each Club, before proceeding. Ideally, someone who is still alive, and preferably someone who is still compos mentis.'

The big Deputy Editor chuckled, presumably because he thought that the words 'compos mentis' were hilariously amusing. Either that, or because he himself was mentally deranged. He carried on. 'We found contact names in various ways. Yours came through the County Cricket Association. Apparently you were Fixture Secretary for a while. Once we'd got that far, we then chased you down through your plumbing business. We aren't exactly detectives, but we do have ways and means. Hope you don't mind?'

'Holy Shit,' spluttered The Plumber. 'You are taking this seriously, aren't you? But having done all that work, I still can't fathom out why you assume that I'm capable of doing it, or that I want to do it. Because I'm not, and I don't.'

Ted Carruthers was a big guy. And he was noticeably sweating. 'Steve, we've no idea whether you'll be any good at this, or not. You may well have limited abilities. In fact, you will, in all likelihood, be absolutely atrocious. But, unfortunately, you are currently the only contact that we've got for Barmfield Cricket Club. So I can only speak to you, can't I? You can recommend someone else if you'd feel happier. That's assuming that you're still in touch with any of them, of course. But if you do that, you'll miss out on a decent fee. We pay quite well here.'

Noting a rather more positive reaction from his now slightly less reluctant visitor, the host kept up the pressure. 'What I suggest is that you do an initial chapter and we take it from there. If it doesn't work out, well so be it. We'll just stop at that point, and give it up as a bad job. However, if we decide that we want you to carry on after that, each chapter will need to be perhaps between one and five thousand words. Grammar and presentation aren't overly important; we can sort that out ourselves, later on.'

Pinstripe Politiko wiped his brow as he continued. 'What we are really looking for is reader interest. For instance, things like humour go down well. And players or officials with strong character traits are also popular. If you can introduce a bit of sex somewhere, even better. The scores and results of any matches need to be as accurate as poss. But it doesn't matter too much if some of the characters get exaggerated a bit. I'll leave all that to you. If you want to lay it on a bit thick, then by all means put in the odd swear word, and we'll make sure that it's AOK before it goes out. Don't worry too much; you can say more or less what you want. We won't get sued, and neither will you. What do you think, Steve?'

The ex-Barmfield Number Two Batsman was now firmly under the spotlight. Some sort of intelligent answer was clearly required. But, lacking somewhat in the IQ department, he hadn't got a clue what to say. This was mainly because he also still hadn't got a clue what Mr Boring Giant had really been talking about.

Luckily the silence was broken by a tap on the door. Coffee appeared, its arrival giving the ex-cricketer much-needed breathing space.

Chomping away at very plush chocolate biscuits from a very plush china plate, Steve Smith tried to understand what had been discussed. Eventually, as some of the Deputy Editor's words finally began to permeate his recently unused brain cells, the Plastic Pipe Expert finally began to become slightly more enthusiastic. Whilst trampling countless biscuit crumbs into the very plush carpet, and spilling most of his coffee over his best, but still not so very plush trousers, he asked another question. As he did so, he noted that the Deputy Editor was frantically trying to clear his desk of important paperwork, presumably because of the confidentiality aspects of Steve's forthcoming task.

'What do you think to this idea, Mr Carruthers? A sixteen-week period more or less ties in with the number of weeks in a league cricket season. So the overall story could be based on the events of a particular year, and each week in your paper could be about one match played in that season. It could therefore all be set in a week-by-week order. And I already have a particular season in mind.' The word 'chronological' had not yet reached Steve's rather limited vocabulary, and no doubt never would.

Ted Carruthers' face lit up. At last he felt that he might not be wasting Percy the Plonking Plumber's time, after all. Or, much more importantly, Ted the Brilliant Ed's. He stopped crawling around his visitor's feet, and put down the plastic brush and dustpan. With bright orange-coloured puffed out cheeks, he replied enthusiastically.

'Steve, that's absolutely bang-on. I'm impressed already. Let's try it like that. Week 1 of your season will be chapter 1 of our article, and so on. But you may choose to do some sort of overview chapter first. It's all down to you. Anyway, please seriously think about whether you are definitely going to do this. I don't want you to say 'Yes' now, and then bottle it later. I suggest that you discuss it with your wife, and then get back to me ASAP. Say by Monday at the latest? Thanks again for coming in, Steve. Speak to you soon.'

As the Ex-Barmfield Cricketer got up from his chair, the previous evening's five pints impacted on proceedings. In retrospect, he should have dealt with his bowel arrangements before leaving home. Unfortunately, due to the time constraints of the ridiculously early 9.30am start, he'd not had chance to do so, and the results of such lack of toiletry action were beginning to take effect. Steve let rip an almighty fart.

Followed by another. As Mr Plumber began to open the door, Mr Pinstripe began to open the windows. Previously meticulously filed antique newspaper cuttings flew in all directions.

As Steve the Perfect Plumber left the room, he took a parting glance at the Deputy Editor. He couldn't understand why the Russian Idiot was scurrying around the floor like some demented imbecile, a bright pink litterbin in one hand, and his nose in the other. 'Blasted Loony', muttered Steve, slamming shut the plush door.

Steve Smith wasn't going back to work now. He was on a high. He scurried out to his van, grinning like a Cheshire cat. He carefully removed the obligatory parking ticket, altered the registration number that had been written upon it, and then affixed it to the windscreen of a nearby ambulance. Before driving off, he searched through various bits of filthy stinking toilet pipes in the back of his vehicle, and found his mobile phone. Wiping sundry faeces traces from the mouthpiece, he rang the day's customer. Luckily she was out, so he could get away with just leaving an answerphone message. Thinking on his feet, he told her that his pet hamster had unfortunately run in front of a passing steamroller, and that he might possibly have to nip it to the vets.

The Urinal Guru drove home, threw himself on the sofa, and began to think about what had been discussed.

For the first time in about fifteen years, the Plumber's grey matter was beginning to function again. In fact, it was moving into overdrive. He wasn't going to wait to hear Whingeing Wendy tell him how totally incompetent he would be at writing anything at all, never mind for a newspaper. He was going to start the Complete Works of Shakespeare Smith before she got home. And then hide the evidence. He began thinking of the people that he used to play cricket with. Several of the old-stagers would be dead by now. Some of the younger ones would probably have grown into big fat replicas of Toadying Ted Crawling Carruthers.

He was sure that he'd kept an important piece of Barmfield memorabilia somewhere. He hurried into the garage, found the stepladder, and carried it up to the landing. He climbed eagerly into the roof.

After half an hour of swearing, through impenetrable dust clouds, at spiders, dead starlings, rotting old plumbing invoices, woodlice, a mouse corpse that smelt like vinegar, and boxloads of Whingeing Wendy's completely useless old university files, he found what he'd been looking for. Almost unbelievably, he really had found what he'd been looking for. This hadn't happened on any of his previous sixty-eight visits to the loft. It was amazing. Such an achievement was a very good omen indeed. Steve Smith could now get properly started on his cricketing memoirs.

Before leaving the roof, he took advantage of being adjacent to the house pipework, and carried out his normal meticulous regular plumbing maintenance regime. Having smashed the ballcock with his roof sledgehammer and given the overflow tank a couple of hefty kicks with his size elevens, the ex-Barmfield cricketer then turned off the light, and returned to the lounge. Again he made directly for his preferred thinking space. Flat out on the sofa, Steve Smith carefully clutched his recently regained prize possession.

He flipped through the pages of the document. Totally oblivious to the mouse droppings, dried-out starling feet and dehydrated wasps cascading over the brand new Leatherland Is Us three-piece suite, Steve was reminiscing like an old granny.

The writing was still perfectly legible. The pages hadn't stuck together, or been used as nesting material by the stupid stinking starlings. This little old piece of history was going to make Steve Smith a rich man. He might even create a few non-Evening Gazette masterpieces as well, and retire on the proceeds. Such potential income would certainly shut up Wendy the Miserable Whingebag, at least for a day or two. And, although he would never admit it, particularly to Deputy Editor Ted Carruthers, he was also going to enjoy writing about the contents of Magna Charta, Version Two. He couldn't remember how he'd got hold of the thing in the first place, but such trivialities were of little consequence now.

Steve homed in on the first page of the old cricket scorebook. It was very neatly written, in black biro. He recognised the handwriting as being that of one of the young players, a lad called Timothy Price. Timothy would have been the Club Scorer that year, before he was old enough to play himself. It gave data of a particular April Saturday of some twenty odd years ago. Steve dragged himself upstairs to his office, backhanded the intrusive pile of overdue bills onto the already well-littered floor, and switched on his somewhat outdated Spectrum 48K. He started to type.

Now, what could he remember of that special summer? Who were all the players in the Barmfield team? What did they get up to, on and off the field? Which one of them should Steve base the first part of his work of art upon? And where was the blasted stupid letter 'T' on his blasted stupid keyboard?

Steve started by listing out the Chapters...

1   The Characters
     In The Summertime (Mungo Jerry, 1970)

2   Trainset
     When Will I See You Again (The Three Degrees, 1974)

3   Mick
     Little Children (Billy J. Kramer & The Dakotas, 1964)

4   Bill
     I Can See For Miles (The Who, 1967)

5   Hypo
    Dizzy (Tommy Roe, 1969)

6   Omar
    Out Of Time (Chris Farlowe, 1966)

7   Sexy Sam
    I Want To Hold Your Hand (The Beatles, 1963)

8   Tantrum
    It's Now Or Never (Elvis Presley, 1960)

9   Nutter
    God Only Knows (The Beach Boys, 1966)

10 Janet
    You're My World (Cilla Black, 1964)

11 Vic
    Ashes to Ashes (David Bowie, 1980)

12 Young Tim
    It's My Life (The Animals, 1965)

13 Moaner
    A Whiter Shade Of Pale (Procol Harum, 1967)

14 Biased Bob
    With A Little Help From My Friends (Joe Cocker, 1968)

15 Des
    Best Thing That Ever Happened To Me (Gladys Knight &
    The Pips, 1975)

16 Persil
    Hey Girl Don't Bother Me (The Tams, 1971)

17 Summer Fete
    Keep On Running (Spencer Davis Group, 1965)

18 Dave
    The Last Time (The Rolling Stones, 1965)

19 End Function
    Saturday Night's Alright For Fighting (Elton John, 1973)

'That'll do for starters. Now I'll get on with Chapter One. That should shut Fatso up.' Steve continued typing…

CHAPTER ONE
IN THE SUMMERTIME

THE CHARACTERS

The human race never ceases to fascinate, does it? Despite the fact that we all live on the same planet, and that most of us have two legs, two arms and one head, we are still all so amazingly different. Both in looks and in character. And so it was at Barmfield Cricket Club. They certainly were an incongruous bunch. Players' ages ranged dramatically, they were of a variety of shapes and sizes, they came from different social backgrounds, and their cricketing strengths and weaknesses differed immensely. Many of the team had nicknames that reflected their appearance, interests or abilities. Or, in certain cases, lack of abilities. There is a story to be told about each one of them, and that is the basis of this document.

The other aspect of this tome is that it chronicles a full league season in the life of Barmfield. It describes the ups and downs of each match, and their overall progress within the County Village League. Could they be champions this year, or would they fail yet again?

In normal batting order, the Club comprised:

Dexter Price. Dexter was normally the Club's Number One. Dexter was an honest and straightforward sort of guy, but could be rather blunt in his critical views about the rest of the team. Also, batting was rather like a war zone in Dexter's eyes; he had an extraordinary devotion to protecting his body, his kitbag being something to behold. Dexter was known as 'Des.' Des was a middle of the road sort of batsman, who had no bowling ability. He was the Vice-Captain. Des was also a bit of a walking rulebook.

Steve Smith. He generally batted at Two. He was a fairly shy character, but he did enjoy the dressing room banter, his expertise being winding up his team-mates. His nickname was 'Trainset,' because of his love of steam trains. He was an average sort of player, being a steady right hand bat. He couldn't bowl for toffee. Or for any other item of confectionery, for that matter. He was the Club's Fixture Secretary.

Sindhu Singh. The Kenyan Indian was Barmfield's Number Three, and also a right arm medium pacer. Sindhu was mild mannered and popular. He was also tall and handsome, with film star looks. He was therefore known as 'Omar,' after Mr Sharif. Omar was always well dressed, both on and off the pitch. He had recently got married, and was now considered by all to be somewhat under the thumb.

John Wickham. Coming in at Four, John was a superb batsman, but a complete pain in the backside in every other respect. He was miserable, and hypercritical of his fellow team-members. In accordance with his character, he was known as 'Moaner.' Notwithstanding his claims to the contrary, he was also very much a non-bowler.

The Reverend Peter Maughan was the regular Number Five. Unsurprisingly known as 'Vic,' he was also an excellent batsman, and a nice bloke with it. Vic was generally rather disorganised, was often late, and, more often than not, was also half asleep. The most complimentary description of his appearance would be 'dishevelled.' Vic occasionally bowled gentle looping off breaks.

Chris 'Tantrum' Boyce was the second of the 'proper' all-rounders. Tantrum batted at Number Six, and could bowl very quickly as well. Still only a schoolboy, he was already very aware of his cricketing abilities. He was full of himself, being loud and aggressive. If things went wrong, he quickly shifted into sulk mode, hence his nickname. He was a good player now, but the rest of the team all knew that he could turn out to be a truly brilliant one in the future, if only he'd learn to listen to advice from others. In the winter, Tantrum was a football hooligan, hurling abuse from behind the goal at the local professional Club.

David Jones generally came in around Seven. Known simply as 'Dave,' he was also a top-notch all-rounder, and had previously captained the side for three years, until he had handed over the reins to Bill Whiteside at the beginning of this season. Dave was always polite and pleasant. He had a good job as an accountant, and also a beautiful girlfriend. He was an extremely popular guy.

Terry Cudleigh was the specialist wicket-keeper. More often than not, Terry went in at Number Eight. A big hefty chap, he was a first-rate batter and stumper. But Terry always had minor medical problems to grumble about; hence he was known as Hypo.

Bill Whiteside. The Team Captain. A supremely positive and bright sort of bloke, he was unfortunately an absolute clown at the playing aspect of the game of cricket. He normally batted at Nine, although Number Thirteen would have more accurately reflected his ability. However his astute brain made him an excellent Skipper, and a very popular one. He was generally just known as 'Bill'.

Michael Fork batted Ten. Known as 'Mick,' he was of the older generation, being both gentlemanlike and courteous. He had been a superb left arm spinner in his time, and could still win them the odd game, despite his advancing years. Mick was the guy who did all the work at the Barmfield ground.

Patrick O'Broughton was usually last man. Patrick was more commonly known as 'Nutter.' He was of Irish descent, and unfortunately wasn't overly bright. Not that the two things automatically go together, of course. He was a typical tearaway right arm fast bowler, and when he occasionally did manage to put the ball in the right place, Barmfield tended to win. He was a drain-clearer by trade. Stories from Nutter about his job amused some of the team, but made others feel slightly queasy. Particularly if recounted after several pints at the pub.

There were sundry 'fringe' players, who occasionally filled in when 'the main men' were not available. Or, in Tantrum's case, were down at the nick. Occasional friendly matches did give certain regular team members a break, and also gave the Club the chance to try out one or two of the youngsters. But in this particular season, reserves were not required for any of the League matches. The regulars were very, very, keen on their cricket, and family holidays were arranged not to coincide with the best game invented by man. And this year Tantrum also managed to keep out of trouble most of the time. This document refers only to Barmfield's League matches, and therefore only to the regular eleven participators described above.

The general standard of the playing staff was very high. Omar, Moaner, Vic, Dave and Hypo were all top class club players. In his younger days, Mick had also been at a similar level, possibly slightly better. Tantrum could end up being the best of the lot in the future, if he could get his brain into gear. So only a few of them were what one would term as of 'average' standard. Captain Bill was the only genuine non-cricketer.

Apart from the players themselves, there were other associated characters:

Bob Jones was the regular umpire. He was Dave's Dad, and was married to tea lady Janet. His main love in life was not his wife, but Barmfield Cricket Club. Now sixty-five, he had years earlier been the best batsman in the area. Unfortunately his umpiring decisions were becoming more and more erratic as the years passed by. Even more unfortunately, many of his decisions had a pro-Barmfield bias, and several of the other teams were now becoming increasingly unhappy with this fact. Bob had therefore gained the extremely problematic name of 'Biased Bob.' Another problem was that Bob had now generated a rather weak bladder, and so had needed to become adept at quickly nipping to the loo whenever there was any sort of break in proceedings.

Timothy Price was Des Price's son. He was fourteen years old, and still very shy, in particular where girls were concerned. Tim was the scorer. The Barmfield lads all considered him as potentially a future player, but, as yet, he'd shown no great interest in this aspect. On the face of it, he just needed a bit more confidence, but he was unlikely to get it from his father, who still took a rather old-fashioned disciplinarian attitude with his eldest offspring. Timothy was simply known as 'Young Tim.'

Samantha Smith was Dave's girlfriend. As a couple, they clearly both got on very well; not only with each other, but also with everyone else. Samantha was known as 'Sexy Sam,' due to her looks and her friendly attitude with her male admirers at the club, of which there were many. Sexy Sam was Barmfield's senior tea lady, and she was very good at her job. She would occasionally also help with the scorebook, if Young Tim was unavailable.

Parvar Singh had recently married Omar. This relationship seemed a bizarre one, her character being totally different to that of her husband. Whereas Omar was easy going, fun loving and unambitious, Parvar was the complete opposite. She had become known as 'Persil' because of her fastidiousness for cleanliness, particularly with regards to Omar's cricket kit. As far as the other players could see, Omar was the only one in the Club who actually liked the obnoxious Mrs Singh. And what she herself saw in Omar, no one could fathom either.

Janet Jones was Bob's wife, and Dave's Mum. Janet was a couple of years younger than Bob. Since her husband had taken up umpiring, Janet had become one of their regular tea ladies. She was very popular, in a motherly sort of way, always being pleasant towards all concerned. Typically of her age group, she had never worked for a living, and so was much more used to spending time in her own company. She was therefore a rather shy, quiet sort of person. She was known simply as 'Janet.'

So these were the main characters. As previously stated, there were a few friendly matches scattered over the season, but in the summertime, the main raison d'être was to win Division Two South of the County Village League. Barmfield were to play 16 competitive matches, and a summary of each one is accounted here.

We start at the beginning..........

'Well, Steve, thanks for coming back to see me,' said the Deputy Editor. 'I've flipped through what you've written so far. It sets the scene OK, but it doesn't exactly say a lot, does it? In fact, one could say it's a bit bland. What's your own opinion of it, Steve?'

The hairs rose on the back of the Plumber's neck. This time he was virtually awake, and he was ready to give as much as he got. He retaliated, in something of a huff.

'It's the best that I can do for the first chapter. Unless I really go to town and slag everybody off, big time. And I'm a bit bothered about doing that, in case some of the team are still in the land of the living. There is a slight possibility that one of them might even read it. I know that's unlikely, given that your newspaper is the biggest load of garbage that the human race has ever set eyes on, but it's still possible, isn't it? When I came here last time, you said that I could write what I wanted, and that your stupid cohorts would sort it out later. Now you seem to be changing your tune. What a flipping surprise that is. If it's not good enough, you can do the whole pointless exercise yourself. I'm off. Goodbye, Mr

Carruthers.'

Steve Smith got out of his seat, and began to make his exit. But the big host moved quickly to stop his visitor from leaving. He beat the ex-Barmfield Fixture Secretary to the door, and physically barred the escape route. He had a big ugly grin across his even bigger uglier fat face. And he was sweating profusely.

'That's more the spirit that I'm looking for, Steve. I knew that you'd got it in you somewhere. Now, try to transfer that passion into your writing. Let's sit down again shall we? And please keep your hair on. What bit you've got left of it. Which isn't much. Anyway, what you've done so far isn't that bad. It just needs more sex and drugs and rock and roll, that sort of thing. As I said before, we can improve it here, after you've done your bit. But we have to have something to improve in the first place, don't we? Please carry on with it Steve, but just try to make it lively and interesting to other people, rather than it just being Steve Smith's boring old life history. And please don't forget that we're paying you well for these articles.'

Somewhat confused with the mind games being played out by his host, Steve Smith reluctantly sat down, and the Deputy Editor carried on.

'It may be that we choose to completely rewrite this first chapter. Or we might decide to roll it in with your second one. But at least you've got the ball rolling, which is the most important thing. So I'm reasonably happy so far, if you are. Well, 'happy' is probably the wrong word, as I'd have preferred it if you'd produced something slightly more interesting, rather than the dross that you've come out with up to now. But we need to make some progress, rather than just sitting here waffling on. So I think the best thing is to leave this first chapter exactly as you've written it, in order that you can concentrate your time on the next one. But, for Christ's sake, Steve, spice it all up a bit. In fact, spice it all up a lot.'

Steve Smith was lost. On the one hand he was being told that his writing was dross. On the other, he was being told that it was good enough for him to continue. He wanted to thump Old Politburo in the teeth. But he needed the money, and a bit of street cred wouldn't go amiss, either. The visitor came to a conclusion. Mr Ted Carruthers was off his trolley, and it wasn't Steve Smith's problem that the cretinous moronic Tub of Russian Lard had flipped his stupid lid. Perhaps he was one of those people with a split personality defect. He was certainly fat enough to be divided into two normal-sized people. The Toilet Expert decided that he might as well just humour the overgrown imbecilic nutcase. Steve relaxed, smirking to himself. He'd got over the starting line, and he could now move forward. And, more importantly, get paid some dosh, as well. So he chose to disregard what had previously been said, and to reply with a more willing attitude.

'Thanks Mr Carruthers. That at least gives me the confidence to get stuck into it. My plan is to produce a couple of dross chapters each week. So it will take me perhaps eight or nine weeks in total. I can't really do it any more quickly than that, or my Plumbing business will suffer. Each of these chapters will represent an inordinately dross Barmfield cricket match, and each will also feature a particular character from the club. So the first load of dross will be about our first League match, and will be based on me. You've no doubt already noted that I was known as Trainset. The second chapter will be about the next League match, and I think I'll base that one around Mick, who was our dross groundsman. And so on. Is this the sort of thing that you're looking for, dross-wise?'

Stupid Fat Nutcase replied. 'There's no need to get on your high horse, Trainset. I mean Steve. Apart from the overuse of one particular five-letter word, it all sounds champion to me. Better than I'd hoped, to be honest. But I must stress that time is of the essence, so I'd be happy if you just get it 90% right, and then hand it over to us. On reflection, perhaps 20% correct is a rather more realistic assessment, in your case. But, joking aside, it's better that you keep feeding it through, rather than trying to make it perfect, because we'll almost certainly decide to alter something. In fact we'll doubtless alter the whole drossing lot of it. But, putting all that on one side, I'm now happy to give you a contract to do this work for us, assuming that you are?'

Steve was by now purring with delight. 'Great. I'll crack on with it then. Just thinking about things, though, I might have to add in the odd other chapter here and there, if that's OK. For instance, I might want to write something about the End Of Season Function, or about the Village Fete.'

'All agreed, Trainset. Er, Steve. Keep in touch. See you in a few weeks. And please bear me in mind, whilst you are doing your writing. The thought of my big fat ugly sweaty face should hopefully create a bit more feeling in your words.'

Steve Trainset Smith left the newspaper offices. He was now in an unusually good mood. But he couldn't understand why he'd not been offered coffee and biscuits this time. Or why the meeting had taken place in the rather downmarket store room adjacent to the gents. Or why Lenin Mark Two had opened all the windows, and had spent most of the time inhaling deeply. Steve Smith wondered if the changes in meeting format were because of the top-secret nature of what he was being asked to do. Walls had ears, and all that. This secrecy element made him feel yet more important.

The Plumber drove away, to sort out Mrs Fitzwilliam's drainage problems. No longer was he the moody, miserable, beer swilling, git of a week or so before. There was a purpose to his existence again now. Lager would take a back seat for a few weeks.

The next evening, Steve Smith turned on his computer and started in earnest. Over a can or two of lager, of course. Things were good, even more so because Mr Ted Carruthers would now leave him alone for a few weeks. He started typing. This time it was for real. It was to be about the first match of the season...

CHAPTER TWO
MATCH ONE

WHEN WILL I SEE YOU AGAIN?

Steve Smith usually batted at Number Two. He had acquired the nickname 'Trainset' a couple of years previously, because he had once mentioned his love of steam trains. In retrospect, this was a fatal error on his part. His guess was that most of the other blokes in the club also liked trains, and probably also cars and planes and boats as well, but they hadn't been stupid enough to mention the fact. He considered himself to be masculine and sporty, but now, unfortunately, his team-mates did not. They thought of him to be some sort of freaky geek. Or was it geeky freak? Why hadn't he kept his mouth shut? Anyway he was now stuck with 'Trainset,' like it or not. The steam-obsessed batter was the Club's Fixture Secretary.

A Plumber in the week, Barmfield Cricket Club was Trainset's life during summer weekends. He'd not been particularly adept at the game when he was at school, and many might say that he'd not improved much since. In fact many did say that he'd not improved much since. Quite often. But he'd found himself playing club cricket through being invited to do so by soccer-playing mates, and he loved it. He'd played since he was 22, and he was now 27. Each year he'd improved a little bit. He was now a regular opening batsman.

The first game of the season was nigh. Trainset was keenly looking forward to five months of playing the best game in the world. Bill Whiteside had taken over the captaincy from Dave, and Des was to be Vice-Captain this year. Trainset had been appointed Fixture Secretary, so he'd been involved quite a lot over the winter, but playing the game is what he liked best.

Away from cricket, the Fixture Secretary had never been very good with girls. He had gone through his school years and his college days without ever finding a regular girlfriend. There had been the odd dalliance here and there, but nothing that lasted more than a day or two. His lack of sexual experience was no doubt one of the reasons why he enjoyed his sport so much. It was a fair bet that he used golf, soccer, squash, tennis and cricket as some sort of psychological compromise to 'being normal.' Whatever 'being normal' is. So the fact that he turned up with a girl by his side for their first match of the season must have come as quite a shock to the rest of the team. And a great opportunity for a bit of banter.

Sue Taylor was what most people would describe as 'Miss Average.' Trainset thought the world of her, of course. But he was looking at her through star-crossed eyes, wasn't he? Probably because she was the only female that had ever taken any great interest in him, other than his Mum. The rest of the human race would see Sue as a five out of ten sort of girl, whereas he saw her as an eleven. She had light-brownish hair, and a reasonable figure. She was tall, perhaps five feet eight or nine, but her height wasn't a problem, as Trainset was over six feet himself. They'd look good together in a wedding photograph. Well, Trainset thought so anyway. In his opinion her face was lovely. He suspected that others would perhaps have called it slightly matronly. Beauty is always in the eye of the beholder, isn't it?

Sue was twenty-five, a couple of years younger than her cricketing boyfriend. She taught French at a local secondary school. They'd met during the winter. It was one Saturday night in the pub. He'd been playing soccer, and had got sufficiently drunk afterwards to ask her out for a drink. And they'd been together, albeit on a fairly casual basis, ever since. Sue said she'd come along with him to a cricket match. So on this day she did.

It was the end of April, and a cold blustery day. Barmfield were away at Elbaston, another village about ten miles further east. Trainset had informed the others that he'd go directly there, picking Sue up en route, because she lived over that way herself. Although he was happier to be turning up with a girl by his side than he would have been without one, he was still somewhat in trepidation about what would emanate from the mouths of his cricketing mates. There were bound to be a few comments from the blokes. Being realistic, there were bound to be lots of comments from the blokes. His expectations were immediately proved to be not unfounded.

Trainset and his girlfriend got out of the car. Sue wore practical clothes on such a cool afternoon. She was dressed in a patterned brownish woollen jumper, and dark brown trousers. To prevent her hair from blowing around in the wind, she had it tied back in a large hair clip. Her brown eyes were framed by only minimal make up. Her shoes were fashionable, but not overly so. Trainset felt that she'd dressed absolutely perfectly for an early season cricket match. He was impressed that she hadn't turned up wearing something stupidly inappropriate, and he had told her so during their journey to the ground.

Most of the others were already there, standing around in the car park. Mick introduced himself first. Mick was the 'gentleman' of their team, and a genuine, old-fashioned, sort of chap. 'My name's Mick. I take it that you're Sue? Pleased to meet you, Sue.' He held out his hand. Sue shook it, in a feminine but sensible manner. She replied. 'Hello, Mick. I understand that you're a good bowler?' Trainset noticed that Sue appeared to be very comfortable in this situation; there was no shyness, or reluctance to talk to the Barmfield groundsman. And he was also very pleased that she'd appeared to remember the pre-match player briefings.

So far, so good, thought Trainset. But unfortunately Moaner was now heading their way. Moaner had this peculiar habit of diving in at the deep end. Moaner looked at the Fixture Secretary's girlfriend, and went immediately on the offensive, as usual. He opened with a question to the female teacher. 'Hello, Sue. Are you insane?' he queried.

Moaner's comments inspired some of the others, and the badinage rapidly degenerated. Tantrum, the tearaway teenager, queried Sue's eyesight. And Omar, who was Trainset's best mate at the club, was next to join in the fun. He came out with a well thought through contribution. 'We expected someone with four legs, and udders. And a big bell round her neck. So you're a bit of a surprise. Anyway, great to see you, at last. I'm known as Omar.' The Number Three Batsman could get away with that one, because his wife, the horrible Persil, was still in the car.

Sue didn't seem to be either upset, or surprised, by the style of humour. Either that or she was pretending that she wasn't. To her credit she smiled politely and occasionally spoke quietly, but confidently, to the other players. Her relaxed approach gradually helped to take the edge off things for Trainset. It was as though she'd known exactly what was going to be said, and had pre-prepared herself for it. By the time the players were getting changed, she'd returned to the car 'To warm up a bit,' and most of the blokes had started having a go at Bill. So the Number Two Batsman could now at last concentrate on the game. 'Thank God that's over with,' he sighed, to no one in particular.

Bill led the players out on to the field. Being new at the job of captaincy, and also being thoroughly talentless at cricket, he immediately proved to need more than a bit of a guiding hand from some of the other senior players. They all knew that this situation was going to happen at the first match, but they were still somewhat surprised at quite how appallingly bad he was.

As the new Skipper started to sort out his fielding positions, Vice-Captain Des informed him that it wasn't a good idea to have four men standing within five yards of each other, all of them behind square leg. 'There's only eleven of us altogether, Bill. Perhaps it might be a good idea to spread us out a bit more, instead of us all holding hands on one bit of the field. In any case, you can't have lots of fielders behind square leg, under Law 41.5 of the Laws of Cricket. This refers to Limitation Of On Side Fielders. Under this Law ...'

Mick cut Des off in his stride, by suggesting to the Captain that he had better move from where he was standing at the moment, as he was in a direct line between bowler and batsman 'You'll get the ball up your arse, Bill, if you stand there. I'd go over that way a bit, if I were you.'

Eventually the game actually commenced. Nutter began his normal farcical ten-second approach from just inside the boundary rope, which gave Trainset the chance to casually check that Sue was still in the car. He was a bit nervous that she might have disappeared to the bus stop, in a huff, because of all the earlier repartee. Or that she would get out of the car and stand directly in front of the sightscreen, and embarrassingly delay proceedings. Or, worse still, that she would wander across the pitch itself during play, perhaps to ask him some banal question, such as about the time they would be going home. As Nutter raced in, it struck Trainset that perhaps women and cricket might not be fully compatible. He could see now why he'd never been introduced to some of the wives and girlfriends. Anyway, Sue was still in the car, albeit seemingly fast asleep, so the Plumber could relax for a while.

'Howzat,' shouted Bill, awaking him from his daydreaming.

'Not out,' replied Biased Bob.

Bill queried the decision, confirming that he was appealing for 'leg before wicket.' Biased Bob replied. 'Because, for him to be out leg before wicket, Bill, the ball has to hit him on his leg, in front of those three wooden things. Not in the middle of his blasted bat, a foot outside the off stump. Play on.'

If Biased Bob thought it wasn't out, Trainset mused, then it couldn't possibly have been. Biased Bob had gained a bit of a reputation for giving opposition players out, when they clearly were not. And for giving Barmfield players not out, when they clearly were. But more of that later.

The first over finished. It must have taken Nutter seven or eight minutes to bowl it, what with his fifty yard run up, and various arguments between Bill and the umpires. 'For Christ's sake, it gets dark at nine o'clock,' grumbled Moaner, to anyone who was interested. As usual, nobody was.

'I reckon it might be better if you leave any appealing to the rest of us, Bill, until you've got some sort of clue about what you're doing,' suggested Hypo, from behind the stumps. Bill took the hint, and also the hump. He shut up completely for half an hour or so. In fact Trainset began to wonder if the Skipper might storm off home in a fit of pique. Des temporarily took over the on-field organisation.

Elbaston eventually finished on 179 for 8 after their forty overs. Neither a good score nor a bad one, Trainset thought, as the players wandered off for tea. It had not escaped his notice that Sue had already made her way down to the Pavilion, a few minutes earlier. 'That's strange,' he thought. 'How did she know to do that? Someone must have told her that we take tea at quarter to five, because I didn't.'

Sue joined in fully during the tea break. She was very friendly with everyone. Surprisingly, she seemed to know quite a bit about the game, and so, when Trainset was sure that no one was listening, he asked her about her cricketing knowledge. She answered that her Dad had played a lot when he was younger, and that she'd often gone along with him to matches. She said that she understood the finer aspects fairly well, and that she had acted as scorer for her Dad's team on numerous occasions.

This sounded too good to be true. The Barmfield Fixture Secretary had taken about a million years to find a girlfriend, and then the first one that he found happened to be an expert on the best game in the world. 'There is a God, after all,' he reflected, stuffing down his third Bakewell tart.

Over refreshments, tea lady Janet Jones was particularly friendly towards Sue. Trainset had often been given the impression that Janet quite liked him, and that she would be pleased to see him get shacked up with 'A nice girl.' Well, it was either that, or the fact that she saw Sue's arrival as a golden opportunity to further distance Trainset from leering after Sexy Sam. Or it might have just been an attempt to get Sue helping in the kitchen. But, whatever the reason, Janet made a huge effort on the Plumber's behalf. She treated Sue almost like her own daughter, doing her utmost to make the new female visitor feel welcome. Janet also paid the Number Two Batsman several little compliments along the way. Most of this Trainset-worship went down well with the Fixture Secretary, but he wasn't so keen when Janet started laying it on a bit too thick. Comments like 'He's a bit of a little teddy bear at heart', and 'I think he's got lovely eyes, Sue', were less popular with the Plumber, especially as Omar was about two feet away from Trainset, and was pulling wide-eyed faces at him.

Bill had by now recovered his composure, after his earlier on-field sulking session. 'Right lads. Let's get on with it. Des, you'd better start padding up, it takes you half an hour. You're opening with Casanova.'

Everyone turned towards the red faced Fixture Secretary and roared with laughter. Including both Janet and Sue, which the Number Two could have done without. 'Well, I suppose it's marginally better than Trainset,' he whispered to himself.

Des and Trainset went to the Changing Room. Barmfield were a bit old fashioned in the kit department, and so most of them still used bats and pads provided by the Club. But Des was of the new 'buy it yourself' school. He started attaching an incredible array of protective equipment, including shin pads, thigh pads, arm guards, hip guards, helmet, inner gloves, outer gloves, thumb guard, chest protector, etc., etc., etc. The rest of the players saw no reason for such behaviour. It wasn't as though the batsmen were going to be facing Wes Hall and Dennis Lillee on a ploughed field. Des gilded the lily yet further, by wearing two genital protectors. Trainset pondered about why Des did this. Perhaps he considered his own private parts to be a protected species, or alternatively he believed that double boxing just made him look better endowed to any passing females who happened to be examining his trouser front. On several previous occasions Trainset had thought about mentioning to Des that all this protection could be making the salesman even slower between the wickets than he already was. Or that it would have been simpler to just have bought a suit of armour and painted it white. Complete with a galvanised dustbin lid for his nether regions. But over the years, the Fixture Secretary had decided that, if Des was happy with the way that he did things, then he'd just keep his mouth shut. So, as usual, he just shrugged his shoulders and got on with doing his own thing. Eventually the opening batsmen were ready to go.

Barmfield won the match, fairly easily, by five wickets. Unfortunately, given the circumstances of having his own personal two-strong female fan club, Trainset failed, edging to the keeper for only one run. On the long embarrassing walk back, he was consoled by two facts. The first one was that he was out to a good ball, rather than to his normal method of skying a bad one. The second was that neither Sue nor Janet was watching. The tea lady would no doubt still be washing up, and Sue appeared to be in the loo.

Des got sixty odd, and Vic did likewise. Tantrum fell to a bad umpiring decision and, on his return towards the Pavilion, hurled his bat in the general direction of third man. The length of throw was later measured, using Moaner's site tape, at thirty-two and a quarter yards, which the Barmfield lads believed to be Tantrum's personal record. But, putting his childish behaviour aside, Barmfield had gained a comfortable victory with several overs to spare, and Bill was delighted.

'Well done chaps, the beer's on me.' Although his personal contribution was zilch, he'd still won his first match as Skipper.

The team retired to the local pub, and had a great evening. Sue and Trainset sat next to Omar and Persil, and they chatted away as though Sue had known them all for years. The new Barmfield lady-killer was still getting the odd comment here and there, but he was by now getting much more blase about his relationship with the French Teacher. So when Nutter asked him, in front of about 30 people, if he'd now given up trainspotting for good, he just laughed along with the rest of them, and so did Sue. It had been a good day, and they had won. Trainset just needed a few runs next week, and all would be looking very rosy in his garden. Very rosy indeed.

Trainset took Sue home. As he stopped the car outside her house, Sue spoke first. 'I'd ask you in Steve, but I must have an early night. I'm off to see my Dad at four o'clock in the morning.'

'Never mind, Sue, that's OK,' he replied, trying not to show that he was more than a bit upset.

'Yes, he's up North, in a long-term hospital. He has been for years. He got hit on the head with a cricket ball about twelve years ago, when he was batting. And he's not recovered since. I was there when it happened, and I'll never forget that day. Never.' Thoughts of Des's protective equipment raced back through Trainset's brain. Who was right and who was wrong now?

Sue carried on. 'I like you very much, Steve. In fact it's a bit more than that, to be frank.'

The Plumber kissed her on the cheek. 'When will I see you again, Sue?' he asked, passionately.

The answer was like a pinprick in a balloon. 'You might not, Steve. I came today to see if I can carry on going out with a cricketer, bearing in mind what happened to my Dad. And I can't. I just can't. I don't want you to pack cricket up just for me, because I know that you love it so much. Sorry, Steve, but I don't want to see a cricket bat ever again. Or hear about one. In fact I don't want to be near a cricket pitch. You know what I'm saying, Steve, don't you?'

Trainset knew what she was saying, all, right. 'Why does this always happen to me?' he pondered on the drive home. 'Absolutely typical. Shitting well typical.' The air in the car went rather blue.

By the time he got home, he'd made a decision. Sue Taylor was now an ex. He was going to carry on playing cricket, as usual, but with one slight change. He'd be wearing a batting helmet from now on. Or a naff suit of chain mail, like Des.

A couple of days later, and pleased with his first attempt at impersonating William Shakespeare, Steve Smith continued his publication. Pint in hand, he started the script of the second game...

CHAPTER THREE
MATCH TWO

LITTLE CHILDREN

Michael Fork was the guy who did all the work. He was known simply as 'Mick.' Now in his mid-fifties, he'd been the Barmfield groundsman for many years. Only the older members could remember a time when he wasn't. Mick was now a part-time chemist at a large pharmaceutical company, having recently chosen a semi-retired life. And he seemed to spend most of his spare hours down at the ground. He was recognised locally as an excellent producer of cricket pitches, and many of the other clubs in the area sought his advice on such a specialist topic. Over the years his role had moved from that of providing a good wicket to doing more or less everything else as well. He was now in charge of all things ground-related. And Mick's idea of being 'in charge' was to do the whole lot himself. The only club matters that Mick didn't get involved in were the organisational side, and specific team concerns. Trainset often thought about how clubs could possibly survive without having their own Mick Fork. He knew, putting it bluntly, that they couldn't. The Barmfield players were very lucky to have Mick at their club.

Mick loved being in the fresh air, and his ruddy complexion proved it. Age had yet to take any great toll on him. He was still a big strong chap, who could move cast iron rollers and heavy timber sightscreens as though they were made of cardboard. He was about six feet tall, with a thick crop of greying hair. In his younger days he had been County Seconds standard, as a left arm orthodox spin bowler, and his huge shoulders bore testimony to the fact that he could still get plenty of turn and bounce, even in the twilight of his career.

The players at the club all knew that there would come a time when Mick wasn't going to justify his place in the team, and that such a situation could well cause them huge problems. They had no right to expect Mick to carry on doing work at the ground, if he wasn't also playing cricket. However, as of now, he was still good enough to be selected on merit, and that fateful day was thankfully a year or two away.

Mick was a Granddad. He had two daughters, one of whom lived locally, the other one in Australia. The local daughter had two children, a boy aged nine, and a girl aged four. For their second game of the season, Mick's daughter had requested that he look after the children for the afternoon, as she'd been invited to an old school reunion day, and her husband had to work overtime, yet again. So Mick had got down to the ground at sunrise, spent several hours doing all the necessary jobs, nipped home for some lunch, and then gone on to pick up the kids. He would by then no doubt have been getting rather tired, and he'd got two very active children and a cricket match this afternoon. When he returned to the ground, several of the other players had already arrived.

'What time do you call this,' asked Nutter O'Broughton, in his Irish brogue. 'I thought you were always down here, Mick. We've caught you out again, you lazy English bugger. I've been here for half an hour already.'

Trainset giggled, awaiting a robust response from the senior statesman. Mick wasn't amused, but, being the gentleman that he was, and also being virtually exhausted, he refused to rise to the bait. 'I couldn't be bothered to do anything today, Nutter, so I thought I'd just have a lie-in. Like you always do,' came the sarcastic reply. 'Oh, and by the way, this is Katie, and the one over there, kicking hell out of my sightscreen, is Jake.'

Katie was a pretty little petite blond girl, and she had a much nicer temperament than her brother. She didn't appear as yet to be unduly influenced by his aggressive antics, but Trainset guessed that scenario would soon arrive. As of today Katie wasn't a problem. But her brother most assuredly was.

The players all introduced themselves to Katie, and then one or two of them strolled over towards the little hooligan taking running jumps at the timber-framed structure.

'Hello, Jake,' Trainset ventured. 'Why are you doing that? It cost us a lot of money, that sightscreen did.'

'Get stuffed, you old prat,' came the anticipated unfriendly reply.

The Fixture Secretary had luckily remembered being informed, recently, by one of his workmates, that touching kids was now an imprisonable offence. So he sensibly refrained from clipping the stupid little brat round the ear. 'Nice to meet you as well, Jake,' he lied.

Jake was quite big and strong for a nine-year-old, and had light brown hair. His attitude reminded Trainset of that of a lad who was on a TV documentary a couple of nights earlier. It was a programme about a pleasant bright boy, who'd turned into a complete pest because no one took any great interest in him. So, with these thoughts in mind, Trainset asked the young boy a rather leading question. 'What are your Mummy and Daddy doing today, Jake?'

The TV theory was immediately proved to be correct. 'I don't know and I don't care. I never see them. I'm always at Mrs Phillips' house. She is a child-minder. And stop asking me questions. Are you a poof?'

Proud at his psychoanalysis, the Plumber began to think of ideas that might keep Superbrat amused for an hour or two. While he was doing so, Tantrum chipped in. The football hooligan seemed to instinctively know how to deal with this younger version of himself.

'Trainset's a miserable old fart, Jake. Don't take any notice of him. And I agree with you. He does seem a bit effeminate, doesn't he? He brought a girlfriend along last week, but we all reckon that she was really a bloke in disguise. She was a right ugly cow.'

The Brat giggled. It was clear that he was extremely advanced for a nine-year-old. Trainset, however, was neither impressed, nor amused. Tantrum carried on chatting to Mick's grandson.

'Anyway, forget about Trainset. He's a blooming Mouth Almighty. He's always got some opinion on somebody or other. Pity he can't see his own faults. He's got plenty of them. But it really is better if you don't boot the sightscreen, Jake. You'd be much better off with a football. I'll find you one at teatime, and we'll have a kick-about. And next season you can come with me down to the match, and smack hell out of a few of the opposition supporters. It's much more fun than smashing up sightscreens. Would you like to do that, Jake?'

The nine-year-old had clearly found a friend. Trainset was pleased about that. But he was not so happy about the fact that the friend happened to be 'that stupid ruddy immature blasted Tantrum.' Furthermore, he was unhappy that the teenaged cricketer was now going to be out on the field, having wound up Jake to a yet higher stage of aggression. The Brat would now be left to his own devices, champing at the bit, with even greater thoughts of causing as much mayhem as possible.

The team took to the field, Bill having lost the toss. During the first few overs, Trainset could see that Mick was being constantly distracted by his daughter's offspring. Jake was by now throwing stones at passing vehicles. And Katie had found a squirrel, and was running round the Pavilion trying to catch it, constantly tripping over in the mud in the process. She wasn't being particularly aggressive, just fun-loving. But it was clear, even from fifty yards away, that she'd already torn her new dress.

Trainset heard Mick speak to the Barmfield Skipper. 'This is hopeless, Bill,' he said. 'I need to find someone sensible to look after them. But our tea ladies are too busy, so I'll go and have a word with the opposition. I'll be back in a few minutes.'

Once Mick had explained the situation, the Brialsford team immediately took matters into hand. Their Skipper had brought his wife along, and she gladly took Katie in tow. After a few minutes of walking her around the ground, and explaining about trees and birds and things, they'd returned to the deckchairs outside Stalag 9, and Katie had dozed off in Mrs Opposition Captain's lap.

On his return to the field, Mick spoke loudly, from his mid-off position. 'One down, one to go.' He was obviously hugely relieved. But the opposition Skipper was clearly still having problems with Jake. 'No need to keep swearing at me, son,' they all heard him shout, somewhat annoyedly.

Trainset had an idea about Baby Yobbo. Between balls, he jogged up to Bill, and whispered his plan into his Skipper's ear. Bill responded positively. 'It might work, Trainset. It's at least worth a try. Ask Mick what he reckons.' So, at the end of the over, the Fixture Secretary ran across to Mick, to explain his thoughts. A couple of deliveries later, Mick asked Bill if he could be excused again. The team were all very interested as to whether Trainset's plan would calm down Brat Junior.

Mick spoke again with the Brialsford blokes, and a group of six of them hurried off to the storage shed. Various boxes and bits of kit appeared, and Mick started organising some sort of component-erection party.

About ten minutes later, Mick returned to the field. By now he was clearly physically shattered. But the Barmfield team would now be able to relax, as they all could see that Baby

Hooligan was now in the practice nets, along with five or six of Brialsford guys. But Jake wasn't batting or bowling. He was playing with Mick's recent new toy, and he was obviously loving the experience of doing so. Everyone at the ground couldn't help but notice that Jake was now as happy as Larry. In fact he was whooping with delight. And the opposition lads were getting a bit of batting practice as well.

What was Jake doing? The cricketers amongst you may have sussed that one by now. But for non-cricket aficionados, here's the answer. Mick had always been good at finding bits of kit from obscure sources, at cheap prices. And his latest acquisition, bought over the winter, was an electric bowling machine. A pound to a penny it had cost some county side thousands of pounds, ten years previously. But Mick had recently managed to get hold of it, second hand, for next to nothing. Not many Club players would have seen one before, but Barmfield now owned one. So there was young Jake, standing on a chair, pouring cricket balls into the thing as fast as he could, and aiming the bowling arm at the opposition batsmen. He was in ecstasy.

There were two minor problems. The first one was that Jake seemed to have deliberately locked the machine controls, in order to make the machine produce regular ninety miles per hour beamers, aimed primarily at the opposition batsmen's heads. Which wasn't a particularly good idea, especially as their Number Eleven was very much a 'last minute fill in'. Not only was he partially sighted, but he'd also got a false leg. The other hiccup was that Mick would eventually somehow have to physically extricate Jake from the machine before it got dark. But these were relatively minor glitches. For now the Temporary Deputy Father could relax and get back to the match.

Bill's skippership had improved already, as the other Barmfield players knew that it would. Bill had succeeded at everything that he'd done in life, and he was clearly quick on the uptake. The team had always thought that, after a couple of learning-curve games, he would be the right bloke to lead them forward. He'd never be any good as a player, because his hand to eye coordination was so poor, but he was a good man-manager, and he was prepared to put in the time and effort to make a success of the job. And that's all that the Barmfield lads really needed from him.

The new Captain's bowling and fielding strategies were beginning to work. He now understood what fielding positions were where, and had quickly picked up which of his blokes could bowl, and which couldn't. Trainset was very much one of the latter.

All the earlier child-based commotion hadn't helped Bill much, though. Brialsford did well, amassing 190 for 7 in their forty overs. But Bill's new found expertise had enabled him to accept that Mick shouldn't bowl at all, because his mind was still on other matters. So Vic churned over a few overs of gentle off spin, and picked up a couple of cheap wickets.

It was a very close game. Barmfield almost got the 191 required, falling only 10 short. But they were unfortunately cleaned up just before their overs ran out. Mick was so knackered that Bill shuffled the batting order a bit, and put him in last. But Granddad still failed to disturb the scorers. Or should one say scorer, as Young Tim was doing it all by himself. Dave was the Barmfield batting hero, scoring an unbeaten 59, but he ran out of partners at the death. Tantrum again failed, but was less expressive than on previous occasions; there was no bat throwing today, this time just ten minutes or so of heavy sulking.

As the players were leaving the ground, numerous conversations were all happening simultaneously. Mick thanked Trainset for his bowling machine brainwave. He also thanked the Brialsford lads for looking after the kids. Des praised Bill on his captaincy, Katie asked Mrs Opposition Captain if she would go home with her, and Nutter apologised to the Barmfield groundsman for his rather insensitive pre-match remarks. And Sexy Sam announced that she had managed a quick repair job on Katie's dress, having found her sewing kit in the car boot. There was a bit of a dampener when Jake was heard to ask Tantrum for a complete printed list of swear words used at football matches, but generally things were heading in the right direction.

The only real problem now was that Jake repeatedly asked all and sundry if he could come along to the next home match. Mick and the other team members had to rapidly think on their feet. They told the youngster that the bowling machine was only on loan, and that it would therefore not be available again in the future. Luckily Tantrum didn't drop the rest of them in it, by reminding them that Barmfield had being given the machine by a County Cricket Chairman at a recent cricket dinner. Apparently that particular evening had been highlighted not only by the generosity of the donor, but also by the even greater generosity of Mick's whisky pouring abilities. Mick had cleverly concentrated his efforts on the Chairman's somewhat overused tumbler.

Although they weren't happy at losing, Barmfield had also gained a few cricketing positives from the match itself. Bill now seemed to have some vague idea what he was doing, and Vic and Dave had played well. But the biggest cheer of the day came later in The Noseblower, when Mick promised them that he'd 'never bring the little twerps to the ground again.' He went on. 'At least I won't do until my stupid selfish daughter starts to look after them like a proper mother should do.'

So, in spite of the defeat, the atmosphere in the pub wasn't too bad. All that Barmfield now needed was for Mick to have a day or two's rest, and for them to get back to winning ways the following week.

Trainset speculated that Mick would, as likely as not, sleep well. And that he would be having a strong word with his daughter, and her 'stupid husband' the next day. He would be telling them all about the problems of using child-minders, and how 'little children need proper parenting'. And that 'The World is going down the pan.' The Number Two Batsman didn't necessarily agree with Mick on this point of view, but he also knew that the groundsman was absolutely convinced that he was in the right.

Barmfield were around half way in the League, after two matches.

Plumber Steve was really into it now. Match Three was to be about skipper Bill. And he couldn't wait to get on with that one. And Whingeing Wendy was away on a course, so he could really concentrate fully on his Barmfield epistle. Out came the Spectrum and the Foscastle lager cans. He was off again...

CHAPTER FOUR
MATCH THREE

I CAN SEE FOR MILES

William 'Bill' Whiteside was a very popular Skipper, having taken over from Dave after last season. Bill was in his early forties, and was about six feet tall. He always dressed well, often wearing rather old-fashioned attire, such as a blazer and a cravat. He had the look of a scientist, in that he was thinning on top, with rather a pronounced forehead. Bill had dark blue eyes and quite a strong muscular physique. He always tried to look the part, and to smell it as well. He generally wore a top brand of rather strong anti-perspirant.

Bill was some sort of salesman. To be truthful, no one ever knew what he sold, or whom he sold it to, but he was always informing everyone that he was good at it. He would regularly tell people that he could sell sand to an Eskimo. Or snow to a camel. He played bridge, and chess, and read the Encyclopaedia Britannica for fun. He was a very bright bloke.

He was married to Anne, who would occasionally turn up to fill in as either a tea lady, or as the scorer, should either task prove necessary.

Bill was also an exceptionally positive character. Being pig ignorant about the game never seemed to overly bother him. Sure, he'd get wound up for a while, but he always bounced back, raring for more. His role was very much that of man-management. And he was very supportive of each player, both on and off the pitch. For instance, if he thought that one of them had been badly treated by a poor umpiring decision, he would argue their case for hours on end, despite not understanding any of the Rules of Cricket in the first place. The Barmfield guys were by now all beginning to think the world of him. Apart from Moaner, of course; he only thought the world of himself.

It was the third League Saturday of the season when it happened.

Trainset arrived at about 2PM for a 2.45PM start. It was a home game against Durfield. By now Mick had been there for about 6 hours, preparing the outfield, pitch, boundary rope, scoreboard, changing rooms, car park, deckchairs, tearoom, sightscreens, practice nets and kitbag. He'd got the covers ready in case it rained, and the parasols out in case it didn't. To complete things, he'd also washed the newly acquired batting helmets and put them on the deckchairs for an airing. Why he did all that while the rest of the side just turned up and played their cricket, Trainset would never understand. But Mick just rolled his sleeves up and got on with it.

Des and Moaner had also recently arrived. Mick walked over to join them, muttering something about a particularly interesting weed specimen at deep long off.

Bill's Jag drew up in the car park. As he got out, the others turned towards him. What they witnessed was something of a shock. In fact it was more than a shock; it was a bolt from the blessed blue. But the word 'shock' was, in point of fact, more appropriate than 'bolt'. As was often the case, Bill looked like something out of a museum, what with his bright pinstriped blazer, and his baggy cream coloured trousers.   But his clothing was not the reason for the astonishment that was being generated in the incredulous minds of his audience.

To see someone metamorphose from Coco the Clown one week, to a punk rocker the next, was manna from heaven for Trainset. This was the moment he'd waited 15 years for. His own golden locks were greying and thinning, and had been for years. Back at school his so-called mates were predicting that he'd be 'bald as a coot' by the age of 25.   He'd surprisingly now reached 27, with still quite a bit left, but future hair loss had always been something that he was more than conscious of. He'd even secretly been down to the local nature reserve to examine coots' heads in greater detail. Future baldness was something that his cricketer pals had also occasionally mentioned to him. Perhaps three or four times a match. Each. In fact 'Kojak' had become his reserve name, when 'Trainset' had been through a period of over usage.

But now here, in front of his very eyes, was the perfect opportunity for the Fixture Secretary to get his own back. He was not sure whom he was getting his own back on, but he instinctively knew that he was going to enjoy this day. Enjoy it very much indeed.

Bill locked up his car, and shuffled across, conspicuously slowly, towards the group, trying vainly to appear unembarrassed.   And also trying vainly to delay the inevitable. He had his cricket bag in one hand and his bat in the other.   Trainset never could get the logic behind Bill having his own piece of finest Gunn and Moore willow, as the beloved Skipper would have played just as badly with a Woolworths boy's size two plastic. But ours not to reason why.

'Afternoon, chaps,' Bill stuttered. 'How are we all today?'

There was a nervous round of courteous 'Hellos' between them.   So far, Mick, Moaner, Des and Trainset had kept straight faces.   The Plumber wondered who was going to crack first. His money was on Moaner. He was right.

'Have you done something to your hair, Bill?' queried Moaner, in his usual droll, laconic way.

Trainset instantaneously took an avid interest in the ground under his feet. It was remarkable how exciting a square yard of gravel could suddenly become. He was squirming with anticipation at what he knew was going to follow, but trying desperately not to show it. His shoulders began to move up and down, and his eyes began to water.

Bill replied to Moaner, in a very serious tone. 'I've bought a toupee, Moaner.' Now the Number Two could relax and savour the moment.

'Well I never,' Mick chipped in, 'I hadn't noticed, Bill.'

That was it for Trainset. Tears started to stream down his face, and his stomach was shaking uncontrollably. 'Sorry chaps,' he mumbled, 'I've got a cold coming on. I'm just nipping back to the car for some tissues.'

'Liar,' said Moaner.

Trainset sat in his car, and wept with laughter. This day was going to be brilliant, and it had hardly started yet. Wait until Tantrum and Nutter arrived. Those two were going to have a field day. Six or seven hours of it were a distinct probability. 'Stuff the stupid cricket,' the Plumber said aloud. And he took a deep breath, and hurried back down to Stalag 9 to get changed, giggling like an eleven year old schoolgirl.

That day the Fixture Secretary found the pre-match atmosphere to be thoroughly heavenly. Tantrum queried whether anyone could get batting helmets with hairpieces already installed. Des followed this by suggesting that shares in the Indian carpets could be a good buy from now on. And Nutter came out with 'Do you have to take it off when it rains?' The others weren't sure whether this was a genuine question, or a joke, as they never did understand where Nutter O'Broughton was coming from, but they all laughed anyway. Apart from the Skipper.

Bill was having a bad day, and he also succeeded in losing the toss. By the time the Barmfield team had to go out to field, ten of them were laughing so much that they could hardly walk, never mind run. The other one was trying in vain to pretend that all the mickey-taking was just water off a duck's back, or perhaps more accurately, water off a rug's back. But the rest of them could sense that he wasn't overly happy with his players.

The opposition opening batsmen entered the arena, Barmfield pretended to concentrate more on cricket than crania, and battle commenced.

The score had reached ten when Barmfield's first wicket taking opportunity arrived. Nutter put in a hostile bouncer, which lobbed gently off the splice towards Bill, fielding at second slip.

Bill had two things to do. The first thing was to move slightly forward, the second was to take the relatively straightforward catch. He did the first thing OK. But as he did so, his new headgear appeared to slip over his eyes, and the ball clobbered into his big toe. As the Captain rolled around on the ground, screaming with pain, ten other blokes rolled around on the ground, screaming with hysterics. Trainset couldn't remember laughing so much in all his life. He was lying on his back with his legs kicking at fresh air. He wasn't the only one impersonating an upside-down tortoise; it must have taken the umpires a good five minutes to get the game under way again.

Bill was not amused. He was also adamant that his pride and joy hadn't slipped. 'I can see for miles with it on. I just misread the speed of the ball, that's all. My toupee never moved an inch. In fact it's stuck on with glue, so it's as solid as a rock,' he remarked loudly to all and sundry. Not the comment most likely to generate much sympathy, Trainset thought, as he started shaking again.

Eventually wigs took a back seat role and cricket a front seat one. Barmfield were getting something of a pasting. Not for the first time, Nutter was bowling all over the place. Perhaps more unusually, Mick's left arm orthodox was also being hit around. Durfield were already about 150 for one, off only 28 overs bowled, when Bill decided that something drastic had to be done.

He had clearly made his mind up that he didn't want a

'proper' bowler on at all. He wanted someone to buy him wickets.

However, not one of the ten other Barmfield blokes could ever have predicted what the 'something drastic' was going to be. Bill had decided to bring Bill on to bowl. Yes, you have read that correctly.

The others had witnessed Bill's right arm slow tripe in the nets. He was absolutely appalling. Yet, completely disregarding what had happened so far on that particular afternoon, he had chosen today of all days to give his 'off breaks' a whirl.

Trainset was standing at mid-on. 'Well,' he whispered to himself. 'Bill's got some guts, I'll give him that.' Then, much more loudly, he shouted across to his Captain. 'Good luck, Skip,' followed by 'Do you want me to pass your toupee to the Umpire?'

This remark just about brought the house down. Trainset was sure that his mate Omar had wet his underpants. Omar told him afterwards that he hadn't done, but the Fixture Secretary wasn't totally convinced. However, he chose not to ask for detailed proof.

Bill was determined to shut up the rest of his team. And he clearly considered that getting a few wickets might just do it. He came in to deliver his first ball. He'd chosen his longer, three pace, run up. There was a melee of arms and legs, a bit like a speeded up version of Magnus Pike impersonating a windmill. Or a two-day-old giraffe on a sheet of ice. The ball eventually appeared, from which hand Trainset was not too sure. It floated in a high arc towards the batsman, at about two miles per hour, so slowly that everyone became transfixed with its flight.

'Is it ever going to get there?' Trainset wondered. For one crazy moment he had this stupid thought that Bill might have accidentally bowled his syrup of fig, instead of the ball. But, on checking, it clearly was the latter, as the Skipper's cranium was still sporting what appeared to be a dark brown rodent.

The batsman swiped wildly at Bill's very, very second-rate delivery. Twice. And missed. Twice. The ball rolled gently up towards the stumps, and stopped. 'Bad luck, Skip,' the Fixture Secretary shouted, somewhat unsympathetically.

But his Captain wasn't listening. He was doing a war dance on the pitch. Trainset had missed the fact that a bail must somehow have fallen off, despite being hit by a force equivalent to a sparrow feather against the side of a Sherman tank.

Bill went on to take 2 for 53, from three overs, his best spell ever. But the opposition still mounted up an impressive 235 for 5. Trainset took a good catch on the boundary to dismiss their Number Five. But 236 to win was a massive total for Barmfield to chase. Especially as they could easily lose concentration again, due to the distractions created by their new team member, Mr Toupee Brown.

The players took tea. Biased Bob took another wee break, and Bill applied another coating of all-over antiperspirant. In the tearoom, Trainset sat down next to Omar. He couldn't fail to notice that Sexy Sam was looking stunning, and was wearing unashamedly tight jeans. Bill's wig took a back seat for a minute or two, whilst the Number Two fantasised about the tea lady. 'Christ, she's well fit,' the Plumber sighed to his mate, 'What does she see in boring Dave Smartarse Jones?' He knew the answer to that one, but he just didn't want to hear it.

Omar wasn't so reserved. He whispered back, hitting the nail straight on the head. 'Dave's a great bloke, popular and good at everything. In fact he is just about Mr Perfect. On the other hand, you're not, you balding idiot, Trainset. You've got no charisma, no nothing. In fact, you've got about as much chance of getting off with her as I have with the Queen of Sheba.' The Number Two Batsman tried to visualise Omar and Miss Sheba in a compromising situation. 'Blasted Smartarse Know-All Jones,' Trainset parried, somewhat pathetically.

A voice awoke him from his naughty thoughts. It was Smartarse Know-All. 'Any chance of a hand with the sightscreen, Trainset?'

'Of course, Dave. No problem, mate,' the Plumber replied,

much to Omar's amusement.

The ex-Captain and the Number Two chatted away as they strolled down to the far end of the ground. 'Are you still going out with that girl that you brought to the first match, Trainset?'

'No, we've split up, Dave.'

'That's a pity. She seemed to be genuinely into cricket. I was hoping that she might do the teas for a while. Samantha's getting a bit fed up with doing them. She wants a break.'

The thought of Sexy Sam possibly not doing the teas in the future was an absolute bombshell. Not because she'd been part of the furniture for a few years now, nor because she was a top-flight caterer. But because Trainset fancied her rotten. And now, because Sue and he had split up, it meant that Sexy Sam still had to be there at every home match. There really was a silver lining to Trainset's relationship clouds.

Dave and the Plumber strolled back to the Pavilion, now chatting about the match. And Bill's piece, of course.

'Right lads,' said Bill, for the umpteenth time. 'We need 236. If we get them we could be up to fifth. But don't let's go daft. Let's take stock for the first fifteen overs or so, and keep some wickets back.'

'OK, Skip,' said Tantrum, followed by 'By the way, are you batting in it, Bill?'

'Of course I'm ruddy well batting in it, Tantrum. It's ruddy well permanent. So ruddy well get used to it,' came the reply. 'And you'll be batting at Number Eleven if you don't shut up.'

Des and Trainset strode purposefully out to the middle, aware of more guffawing from the deckchairs behind them.

Des took no notice whatsoever of his Skipper's instructions. He immediately went wildly on to the attack. His strength had always been the short ball outside the off stump, and he was fed a glut of them. So much so that after six overs the openers had already got forty, and Durfield had resorted to two deep third men. Trainset was content to watch, and just push the ball around, while Des got on with it.

Eventually the stand was broken on 81, when Des got a good one, and was bowled for 48. His partner soon followed, skying the balding loud-mouthed medium pacer to long off. He'd made a decent 32, so both openers had given the team a good start.

The rest of the side chipped in here and there, but wickets also fell. Hypo eventually won Barmfield the match, with a gallant 38 not out, including a big six over cow corner. For those readers that don't follow cricket, cow corner is a fielding position, not a loo for Friesians. Bill failed to trouble the scorers, but he couldn't blame that on his new hairstyle, as, more often than not, he failed to trouble them anyway. So Barmfield eventually scraped home by two wickets. Biased Bob hadn't needed to make any important decisions at all, which was another big plus point.

The pub was a great place to be that evening, with both a win and a syrup of fig to chat about. Even Landlord Tom joined in. 'That'll be eleven pounds forty, please, Bill. Do you want your change in cash, or in tubes of Bostik?' Some of the pub regulars didn't recognise the Barmfield Skipper. They seemed to assume that he was the Club's new Australian professional, and that he was a red-hot fast bowler. One of the old ladies even asked Mr Bostik for his autograph.

Trainset thought that this had been one of the best days of his life. He and Omar laughed and laughed all night, even more so when Persil was in the Ladies.

Bill's hairpiece was to remain in service, albeit on an intermittent basis, for the rest of the season. It became noticeable that, if Bill or his team had done well the previous week, he wore it. If not, he didn't, using some sort of excuse for its absence. Like 'Tiddles thought it was a rat; so it's at Wiggie's for repair.' Another one was 'Anne put it in the tumble dryer by mistake, and half the hairs fell out. We had to call in a plumber. We got a decent one, of course. Not Trainset. He'd have buggered up the drains to the whole street. Or set the house on fire.'

Barmfield were now fifth, after three matches. Things were looking up. Could they win the League?

Steve had a few emergency calls to deal with, and Whingeing Wendy was also on the warpath. So several days passed before the Perfect Plumber could get back onto his penmanship. But he was really into it now, and at the first opportunity he was at it again. Looking in the old scorebook, Steve noted that it was now the turn of the ex-wicketkeeper to be torn to shreds. Out came the Spectrum and the Foscastle lager cans. Off he went…

CHAPTER FIVE
MATCH FOUR

DIZZY

Terry 'Hypo' Cudleigh was Barmfield's keeper, and he was a very good one. He was twenty-seven, the same age as Trainset. Hypo had been one of the Fixture Secretary's best mates at school, but they'd drifted apart for a few years, until Trainset joined Barmfield at the age of 23. Coincidentally they'd both ended up being in similar jobs, albeit that they had got there via completely different routes. When he was 16 Hypo had been selected as a County Schoolboy cricketer, and Trainset supposed that it was around that sort of time period that their lives had started to take different directions. As has been previously mentioned, Trainset wasn't very good at cricket in his school days, even though he loved the game. So it seemed a bit weird that he was now playing at the same level as Hypo. The Number Two Batsman guessed that he himself must have improved a bit over the years, and that

Hypo must have lost a bit of interest. But Hypo was still good.

In Trainset's eyes, Hypo wasn't slim. He never had been. In fact, he was bloody fat. Trainset could remember his schoolfriend telling him, when they were about ten, that he 'had problems with his glands.' This sounded deeply plausible at primary school age, and Trainset had believed the story implicitly. But doubts started to creep in during their early teens, when Hypo was seen to spend more time than most in the queue for the tuck shop. He'd even somehow managed to wangle a lunch-hour job actually serving in it, no doubt due to the availability of free crisps and Mars bars.

Hypo was blue eyed, with a mop of rather unkempt hair. He didn't have much of a neck, and to Trainset this seemed to make him look like one of those plastic round-bottomed clowns that are often found in the bottom of a parrot's cage. Trainset liked to pull the leg of most of the players, but Hypo didn't seem to have any legs to pull.

Still, putting his large size and even larger appetite aside, Hypo had always been good at cricket. Wicket-keeping and batting were his forte. Trainset guessed that Rodney Marsh would be the nearest comparison to Hypo that he could think of, with both of them being left-handed batsmen. In his less complimentary moments, the Plumber thought of a Hypo as a sort of Mr Potato Head character, a bit like a beer barrel with wicket-keeping gloves sticking out the sides. But he kept such rather nasty thoughts to himself. Trainset knew that Hypo would never have been any good at bowling or fielding, because of his bulk, but he was absolutely excellent at both batting and keeping.

Hypo was of average height, about five feet nine. He had a mass of brown hair, and was generally a fairly chirpy sort of a character. Because he stood behind the stumps, he was always involved in the game, and he contributed a lot to the Barmfield team effort. He was forever shouting encouragement to the bowlers and fielders, and he was very aware as to what was happening tactically. Like a few others, he was clearly good enough to captain the side, but the rest generally felt that they would get more out of him if someone else took on that burden. So Hypo was just left to do his own thing. The keeper was also fully involved in all non-cricketing aspects of the Club, often arranging various social events.

Hypo was therefore a very popular character at Barmfield Cricket Club. A leading light, if ever there was one.

But, unfortunately, like the rest of the guys in the team, he had characteristics that made him stand out a bit from the rest of the human race. In Hypo's case, his weakness was that he was something of a hypochondriac. He had a penchant for having illnesses and injuries, and for repeatedly telling everyone about them. Over and over again. If he'd got nothing overly serious wrong with him, then he'd still have a series of minor problems, such as 'having a bit of a headache,' or 'desperately needing a drink,' or just 'feeling a bit off.' Although he'd known Hypo for years, Trainset had never got to the bottom of which of this lot were genuine, and which were just part of Hypo's psyche. He occasionally thought that Hypo perhaps needed some sort of problem, just to help him raise his game, like professional footballers did. Or that he had to have something wrong as an attention-seeking ploy. Or it could just have been that his weight was legitimately causing him physical discomfort. Trainset was never truly sure with Hypo.

The real worry for the Fixture Secretary and the others was that one day Hypo might say that he'd got heart palpitations, and that the rest of the side would all laugh it off. And then later wish that they hadn't. Bearing this in mind, the other players were generally fairly sympathetic to Hypo's health issues. And so, by 10PM on Saturday evenings, many of the team often felt that they had become medical counsellors. Well, inebriated versions thereof, anyway. Trainset could remember an excessively drunken Nutter once asking him if 'Heado had got another sodding Hypeache', and this line had now become fixed within the annals of Barmfield history.

Barmfield were away at Belter, about 15 miles away. It

was gloriously sunny. The forecast was that it would be hot all day. Barmfield batted first, and they chalked up a good total. Trainset top scored with 52, Dave hit 43, and Nutter clouted a rapid 22 not out at the end. Of the batsmen, only Moaner failed, being given dubiously lbw by the Belter umpire for a duck. Which went down like a lead balloon, of course. So Barmfield ended up with a good total of 225 for 9.

At tea, Moaner wasn't happy. However, Bill was, even though he himself had been bowled first ball by Belter's Indian leggy. Against faster bowlers, Bill always gave the impression that he would be better off taking a white stick out to the wicket, rather than a bat. But against spinners, he was worse. Trainset had calculated that Mr Hairpiece spent more minutes over the season in taking guard and studiously surveying the field, than he did from that time onwards. Particularly so with spin bowlers, as it was usually all over within ten seconds.

However, getting back to the game in question, the Skipper had sussed out that the wicket was good, and the outfield was fast, and that Barmfield had to bowl and field well to win the match.

Nutter and Omar opened the bowling, and both of them were getting plenty of bounce and no little movement. Trainset had a good view of proceedings, as he was fielding at first slip. Hypo was keeping well. He was always on his toes, reading the pace and bounce, and making keeping look easy, as usual. But it was the hottest day of the year, and after about ten overs, Hypo was, putting it mildly, starting to get a bit warm.

'Any chance of a drinks break, ump,' Hypo asked of Biased Bob.

The reply was negative 'Only when a wicket falls. Let's get on with the game.' The cricket continued, and Hypo was becoming more and more ill at ease.

The Belter openers were batting well, if rather slowly. No wickets had fallen after twelve overs, so Bill made a double bowling change. On came Tantrum and Dave Jones. These two also bowled accurately and quite quickly, but the stubborn openers were proving hard to dislodge. And Tantrum's constant cursing and swearing at batsmen and umpires had no effect either. The score had crawled to 38 for nought, after 14 overs. And, until Barmfield got a wicket, Hypo knew that he couldn't have a drink. He was starting to boil, both physically and mentally. Trainset was standing next to him, so he could hear and see it all. It was one moan after another from the man behind the stumps.

'I'm feeling dizzy,' was followed by 'I've never played in such heat'. Then, omitting the stream of Billingsgate fish market adjectives, Hypo said something along the lines of 'Why was that appeal turned down? It was plumb out.' At the end of the fifteenth over, he started again. 'I'm sweating like a stinking pig, I'll have to take my gloves off.'

Hypo did take his gloves off, along with the inners. Unfortunately it was by now about six o'clock. And, as often happens at that time of day in England, insects had started to take to the air. Precisely at the same moment as Hypo's fingers appeared, so did a swarm of gnats, and they homed in on the keeper's uncovered sweaty palms. As well as on his uncovered sweaty face. Trainset quickly retreated from slip to short third man, to watch proceedings from a safer distance. He never had been much of a hero, insect-wise. From his vantage point, he saw a very large fat cricketer wafting his very large fat arms around as though he was attempting a vertical take off. There were several swear words that the Fixture Secretary had not heard before, along with about thirty or so that he had. It was clear that Hypo was not a very happy chappie.

The first to come to Hypo's rescue was Belter's Number Two batsman. He was also quite a portly chap as well, with a thick greying beard. He joined Hypo in a gnat-wafting operation, which was occasionally punctured by 'Ooh,' and 'Ow' and 'Shit.' One gnat sting isn't much in itself, but fifty or so gnat stings each was a slightly different story.

Biased Bob and the Belter umpire jogged off to find insect repellent. Well, hobbled off would be more accurate, as their combined age must have been well over 150. Trainset mused that, by the time that the two old codgers had got back to the action, it would be dark, and the local pipistrelle bats would have beaten them to it. But the two old fogies did return in reasonable time. After they'd both taken advantage of the break to yet again use the toilet facilities, of course. Luckily the Belter first aid kit had been well stocked, and two cans worth of fly spray was eventually wafting around Hypo and their Number Two. Biased Bob had also brought out a few cans of Bill's antiperspirant spray, just in case.

The sight of this gnat-defence equipment encouraged more of the fielders around to help. In fact, even Trainset himself was by now slightly nearer to the action. Between them they managed to vanquish what was left of the attackers. The Belter Skipper had the wherewithal to bring out trays of drinks, wet towels, and antiseptic cream, in an attempt to further assist the two injured parties.

Trainset looked at Hypo. Not only had he got a big fat bright red face, and big fat bright red hands, but he also appeared to be suffering from chicken pox. One part of Trainset wanted to laugh, another to cry. Hypo looked in such a measly state, sitting on the grass, drinking pint after pint of water, and scratching himself until his skin bled. The Belter Number Two was a yard or two away, generally in a similar condition, although not supping quite so exaggeratedly. And not looking quite so overweight, either. There were a dozen or so cricketers hovering around, from both teams, not really knowing what to say or do.

Dave Jones broke the ice. 'Do you two want to carry on?' he asked them both.

The bearded guy reacted positively. 'Of course we do, we're not going to let you lot beat us. I'm ready to bat. Let's get on with it.'

Hypo was slightly less enthusiastic. 'If we must. But can I have couple more pints of water, first?' This was followed by 'And a Mars bar, or something similar.'

Bill told them both to take their time, and that there was no rush. In the background Trainset, and several of the other fielders, heard Moaner mutter something along the lines of

'What's up with the modern generation? In my day we wouldn't have stopped the game for a few piffling little fleas. It's totally unsatisfactory, in my opinion.' But no one took much notice of Mr Miseryguts; they were all much more pleased that the game was about to restart, still with eleven on each side. Well, ten and a half on each side, to be more accurate.

The game got under way again. Trainset took up his place at first slip. And, from his nearby position, he had to fully give Hypo his due. Despite the injuries, and perhaps more so his embarrassment, he still kept wicket superbly. Albeit that every delivery was followed by 'I could do with another ruddy drink,' or 'When does this stupid match finish?', or 'What is the point of blasted insects, anyway?' Whilst watching on, Trainset thought about why Hypo was so good behind the stumps. He concluded that it was because it all came so instinctively to the Barmfield stumper. He had this ability to be able to spend all afternoon concentrating his mind on other things, such as his various illnesses, without it having any adverse effect on his wicket-keeping performance. When Nutter sprayed them way down the leg side, Hypo was already in the right position, and the ball would slap into the middle of his gloves. It was because of this inbuilt ability that Trainset had always considered Hypo to be a superb player.

So, although he was constantly whingeing to all and sundry, Hypo still took a couple of admirable catches, and a peerless stumping, and Barmfield went on to win the game. Most neutral observers would say that their match-winner that day was Mick, who turned Belter over for 145. He took seven for 48, a superb spell of spin bowling on a flat, easy paced wicket. He certainly rolled back the years with that performance. But Trainset's personal 'man of the match' vote went to Hypo. Apart from the minor downside of having to put up with a three-hour long ball-by-ball running account of his injuries and illnesses, in the bar afterwards, Trainset felt that the keeper had been brilliant.

It was another win for Barmfield. As Bill applied another coating of antiperspirant, he mentioned that he thought they'd now be up to fourth.

'Well done Hypo! You were a real hero that day'.

Steve giggled to himself. His wife was out, so he could talk aloud without her accusing him of being an imbecile. 'That's Hypo dealt with. Now I'm going to give Omar a bit of a slating. All this is really good. I'm enjoying doing it. That Big Fat Tub of Lard at the Evening Gazette is going to be impressed with what I've done. I reckon that I should have gone into the publishing world, rather than forever sticking my head down Mrs Brownarse's outlet pipe. Perhaps Fatso will give me a job as his right hand man'.

A couple of days earlier, Steve had left a message with the Newspaperman's secretary that he was on programme. He'd deliberately phoned at lunchtime, so that he wouldn't have to speak to the Sweating Russian Idiot. And he'd permanently set his phone on 'messages only' for the last couple of weeks. Steve's confidence was higher than it had ever been before, and he didn't want any interruptions. He couldn't believe how well he was doing all this. Anyway, back to Omar…

CHAPTER SIX
MATCH FIVE

OUT OF TIME

Trainset considered Sindhu 'Omar' Singh to be a great bloke. The all-rounder was pleasantly laid back, and very popular. Kenyan by birth, he had lived in England since he was ten, and he was now twenty-four years old. He was tall, with Omar Sharif film star looks, hence the nickname. He was dark skinned and very athletic. He worked as a junior office manager at a local textile factory. An excellent batsman, Omar had arrived at the club via the County Schools and local University First elevens. He had topped the Barmfield batting averages for three years in succession. Trainset reckoned that Omar could have gone on to play high level cricket, if he'd chosen to. But Omar was happy with his lot, and thoroughly enjoyed his summer afternoons with Barmfield.

Omar was very 'European' in his dress and in his attitude.

Until he met Persil, he lived with his mother in a fifteen-storey high inner city block of council flats. His Mum was a very traditional Kenyan Indian, her normal mode of dress being a sari, or similar. Omar's Dad had died many years earlier, and his brothers and sisters had long since left home. So Omar had a bit of an ongoing problem in trying to live his own life and also look after Mrs Singh Senior. And this situation could only get worse now that he'd moved out to settle down with Persil.

Omar was the Plumber's best mate at the club, particularly so because they both enjoyed a pint or two. Omar was Trainset's regular drinking pal. That is, he was Trainset's regular drinking pal until he met Persil. In Trainset's view, Persil had inspired an immediate detrimental effect on his best mate. She had seemingly taken over his life, and Omar had become obsessed by her opinions and attitudes. They had met towards the end of last summer and had got married during the winter.

Barmfield were again at home, this time against Borrowater, normally a middle of the table outfit. For the first time ever, Vic had brought along his two sons, 'for a bit of fresh air.' They were about six and three years old respectively, and both of them already sported the hangdog presence of their father. Vic's pre-match instructions to them were 'Stay with the adults' and 'Be nice to everybody.'

Des and Trainset opened, as usual. They began the walk to the middle, to a few sporadic claps from the deckchairs.

They went through the normal charade, Des asking the same question that he'd asked fifty times before. 'Which end do you want, Trainset?'

The Fixture Secretary had played with Des long enough to give the right answer. In reality what Des meant was 'I'm better than you, Trainset, so I'm taking the bowling first.' So, as usual, Trainset's reply was a diplomatic one. 'You face the first ball, Des, and I'll watch from the other end.'

Des was happy, which was always a good starting point to the game.

The fact that Des was 'better than Trainset' didn't seem to

unduly influence matters that day. Des sliced the first ball of
the match over gulley's head for a fluky boundary, played and
missed at the next four deliveries, and had his off stump
uprooted by the sixth. The opposition went wild. Trainset
was sure that their fast bowler thought that he'd just cleaned
up Boycott. Four for one. Barmfield were in trouble already.
As Des walked past his thinning haired opening partner, he
uttered a soulful 'Sorry, Trainset.'

Even though Des could sometimes be a complete pain in
the arse, Trainset genuinely liked the bloke. And he hated to
see him so upset. The Number Two tried to put on a positive
face. 'Never mind, Des, it's Wollatown next week.'

Out marched Omar. Looking completely immaculate, as
usual. Trainset reckoned that his missus must have spent
every Friday night, all night, ironing his kit. Or perhaps she
just bought a completely new set each week.

The game moved on a few overs, to a score of fifteen for
one. Trainset had hit one of his trademark 'tennis shots'
through mid wicket. Omar had belted a cracking off drive to
the boundary. Things were starting to improve a bit.

The Borrowater opening bowler stormed in. He pitched
the ball well up, on off stump. The Fixture Secretary played it
back past him. He'd hit it in the middle. It felt good. But
Omar was not overly interested in Trainset's WG Grace-like
effort. For some unearthly reason, he was staring across
towards the deckchairs, apparently checking that Persil was
still happy with his appearance. Trainset instinctively knew
that Omar wasn't remotely aware that the bowler had
delivered the ball. The straight drive hit Omar on the inside of
the ankle, and ricocheted past the balding loudmouthed fat
bloke at mid-off.

The rebound meant that there was now a chance of a
quick run. Not realising that his batting partner was genuinely
injured, the Plumber called 'Run One, Omar.' And he raced
down the pitch.

The Number Three Batsman woke up. He shuffled a
couple of yards towards Trainset, stopped, attempted to hop
back to his crease, and gave up. Sensing that there might

just possibly be a potential problem looming, the Plumber applied the brakes. Omar stared back at him, somewhat forlornly.

By now the balding loudmouthed fat bloke at mid-off had galloped back ten yards, and was hurling the ball towards their keeper. To be more accurate, he'd lumbered slowly after it, and was weakly propelling a rather effeminate underarm lob in the general direction of the chap wearing big gloves. But with Trainset now chatting away mid-pitch to a completely desensitised sack of sweet Kenyan potatoes, fifteen yards nearer Omar's end than his own, there was no point in trying to get back to his crease. On reflection, the Fixture Secretary later realised that he should have carried on running past Omar, so that at least one of them would still be out there. But, in that split second of time, Trainset just didn't appreciate that Mr Sweet Potato-Head would not now be playing any further part in the day's proceedings.

'Owzat' screamed the stumper, exultantly. Even Biased Bob was struggling to give that one 'Not Out'. And he couldn't call 'No-Ball', as he was at the wrong end. He was stuffed. And so was Trainset. Omar sheepishly looked at his batting partner, and then came out with what was later to become a classic line.

'Sorry. Did you say something, Trainset?'

The reply was not friendly. 'Oh, for Christ's sake, Omar, you idiot. Of course I effing well said something. I called you for a run. But you weren't listening. As usual.' The Plumber trooped off towards the deckchairs, muttering curses about Kenyans, Indians, Chicken Tikka Masala and gastroenteritis.

'Bad luck, Trainset,' shouted Bill, encouragingly. 'But there's always next week. It's Wollatown.'

The deckchairs went quiet, awaiting a dramatic response from the Number Two. They all thought that it wouldn't be long before Trainset screamed something along the lines of 'Stuff next week, you bald prat. And stuff the week after as well. I hate effing stupid Indians.' And then follow it up with 'And why are you wearing that twopenny-halfpenny bit of Persian carpet on your head, Bill?' In other words, they expected the opener to respond like any self-respecting premiership footballer would, to a match day official from the Far East.

But what came out was just a predictable stiff upper lip typical cricketer comment, 'Sorry Skip. My fault. Not to worry.' The deckchairs relaxed. And Vic's two young sons could remain virginal in the swear word department. Well, they could for a few minutes longer, anyway.

Trainset stormed into Stalag 9, sat down, and sulked. Through the tearoom window he could see stupid half-baked ruddy Omar hobbling towards the pavilion, being helped off by the bowler with the ponytail and by the bloke that looked like the drummer out of Led Zeppelin. The loudmouthed Persil was already out there. Trainset wasn't sure whether she was giving Omar a helping hand, or examining his trouser bottoms for possible insurance claim damage. Trainset also noticed Biased Bob jogging towards the pavilion, presumably en route to the bog.

As Omar crawled through the deckchairs, the Fixture Secretary could hear Bill trying to remain positive. 'Bad luck, Omar. Not to worry, old boy. You'll be OK in half an hour. In any case, it's Wollatown next week.'

Fifteen for two, and Omar needing a runner. Or an ankle operation. Not the greatest start to a game. And, worst of all it was Wollatown next week. Barmfield couldn't possibly face their local rivals on the back of a big defeat. Bragging rights would be one-way traffic. They had to win this match.

Trainset leant out of the window. Nearby was the long leg fielder, a horrible looking spotty bloke, with a moustache that looked like a dead baby rat. He obviously hadn't realised that the Number Two Batsman was behind him. 'Well, that's got rid of two more of the prats,' Mr Spotty addressed, just loud enough that the deckchairs couldn't quite hear him. But, being a bit nearer than they were, Trainset did, and he took it all in, big time.

The Plumber watched Moaner step across the boundary rope. If the batting side ever needed a trademark innings from Moaner, it was now. The Number Four looked focussed and determined.

Vic was also rapidly putting on his pads. Well, as rapidly as Vic ever did anything. Which wasn't very rapidly at all. His two boys weren't helping, either. They seemed to be asking their father every possible combination of every possible question that the world had ever thought of, all at the same time. Whilst crawling around between their father's feet.

'Good luck, Moaner,' shouted Bill. Followed by 'Get a move on Vic, for Christ's sake. Or you'll be out of time.'

Being given out 'Timed Out' is quite an unusual event in cricket. Particularly in local cricket. But with Vic, Tantrum and Dave Jones all trying to pad up together, it very nearly became a reality. Trainset later thought that the only reason that the opposition players didn't appeal to the umpires, was because most of them were too busy laughing. The only one seriously concerned seemed to be Des, who was avidly reading Law 31 of the Laws of Cricket, in order to check where everyone stood contractually. He was particularly interested to find out whether the fact that the fielding side were rolling around on the grass, unable to speak, meant that they could be considered at least partly responsible for any delay.

Tantrum was in the middle of the deckchairs, imploring the prostrate Indian Number Three Batsman to remove his right pad, even though Omar was convinced that it was actually the only thing connecting his ankle to his leg.

'For f...'s sake, Omar, I need your f...ing pads.' Tantrum started pulling at the pad on the injured leg. Omar wasn't impressed. 'Get off Tantrum, you prat. Ow. You stupid moron. I said ruddy well get off.' Persil and Tantrum were by now in a tugging match, stretching Omar in four directions at once, and punching each other as they did do.

During this particular melee, Vic was desperately trying to drown out the swearing, in order to prevent his perfect little offspring from hearing something that they shouldn't. For reasons unapparent to the rest of the players, he began to sing the first tune he could think of, a very loud and out-of-tune version of 'Onward Christian Soldiers.' Having finished that, and on noticing that some of his team-mates were still not complying with all necessary non-profanity requirements, he then followed up with a slightly less uplifting strain, which he'd heard on the car radio on the way to the match. But 'My Ding A Ling' didn't seem quite appropriate for a Vicar, somehow. Well not to Trainset it didn't, anyway.

Trainset found out later that Dave was screaming at him through the toilet door, imploring him to throw his pads out. Unfortunately, it wasn't Trainset who was in the loo; it was Dave's Dad. The Number Two was leaning out of the tearoom window, about 15 yards away around the corner, and he hadn't realised that Dave was talking to him. He just assumed that Dave was shouting to Des; he'd temporarily forgotten that Des had his own pads, and that there was no way that he'd let anyone near his prized possessions. Not even if Barmfield were to be thrown out of the League if he didn't.

While all this was going on, Vic was trying to explain to Bill that he was, in actual fact, right-handed, and therefore couldn't go out to bat wearing left-handed kit. He was doing so between verses of his current number, Rolf Harris's 'Two Little Boys.' And whilst giving his eldest a rather unfatherly clip round the ear.

Just to further confuse things, Biased Bob's stinking sheepdog had taken a fancy to the kit bag, and was scampering around the deckchairs wrapped in an umpire's coat, with Genital Protector Number Two in its slavering mouth. 'And I'm not wearing that box, now, either,' said Vic, somewhat forcefully.

As Vic was ready to go out to bat, everything suddenly went very quiet. The Vicar's youngest son broke the silence by asking the Reverend a final, pre-innings, rather deep and technical, cricket question.

'What's an effing jox trap, Dad?'

Eventually a degree of sanity was restored, and Vic dragged his torso over the boundary line. Complete with an assortment of kit that made him look like a cross between

Linford Christie and Mother Teresa. Biased Bob hobbled out behind Vic, fastening his flies as he did so. Moaner jogged back from the wicket towards Vic, to see what the fuss was all about. Trainset heard miserable Moaner shout out, rather unsympathetically, to his bedraggled religious colleague. 'There's quite a big scuff mark on the track where that run out happened. If their quickie puts it there, he'll knock your stupid halo off, Vic. Followed by your stupid head.'

Well at least Moaner was his usual cheery self, thought Trainset. 'Well done Moaner,' the Fixture Secretary voiced quietly.

Omar joined Trainset in the changing room. The Number Two took one disparaging glance at his supposed best friend, and then stared back out of the window. Words were not spoken. Omar decided to keep his mouth firmly shut.

Moaner and Vic took their respective places at the crease. Well they thought they had done, until the Belter umpire and Captain both began arguing that the two batsmen had gone to the wrong ends. Biased Bob didn't agree with them, and it was another five minutes before cricket took precedence over farce, and battle re-engaged.

Barmfield eventually amassed a total of 187 for 8, off their 40 overs. Not bad, considering where they'd started from. Moaner made a classy 85, including fifteen fours, punched all around the ground. And Bill rattled up his highest score of the season, three not out, including an edge through slips for two. His hair covering stayed on throughout. Tantrum got a few runs this time, meaning that he was slightly more relaxed. And therefore so was everyone else. Omar didn't have to bat again, which was good news all round.

Tea was taken at about quarter to five. As they all sat down, Trainset contemplated his earlier bad fortune. A wicked thought crossed his mind. 'With a bit of luck, Omar could be out for the rest of the season.' He chose to keep that one to himself.

In Trainset's opinion, the food was, as usual, brilliant. He was more of a cold buffet person than a hot meat and veg one, so he always loved his cricket teas. And the beautiful

Sexy Sam was keeping all the blokes inordinately interested in the proceedings. The Plumber was of the view that half of them never really wanted to go back out on to the pitch. The Barmfield players were all much happier now. Apart from Omar, of course. His healthy brown skin had changed to a creamy sickly white. He reminded Trainset of Michael Jackson. And his appearance was matched by his newly found solemn attitude; for the first time since he was four and a half days old, Omar elected to refuse a cup of boiling hot tea. The Opener continued to refuse to speak to the Kenyan.

Omar wasn't fit to participate. Bill led the other nine out to field. As they strolled out in groups of two or three, he tried to rouse them up a bit. It wasn't exactly 'Swing Low Sweet Chariot' stuff, more along the lines of 'I know that we're crap, but we might even win this, if we get a few lucky decisions from Biased Bob. And if Nutter achieves a lifetime ambition and puts it somewhere on the track, for a change.' And, as a final plea to their heartstrings, he came out with 'And don't forget, it's Wollatown next week.'

In came the openers; the horrible looking spotty bloke with a moustache that looked like dead baby rat, and who Trainset now hated with a vengeance. And his partner, 'Fred,' the wicket-keeper. Fred was well known in local cricket circles, both as a big hitter and even bigger beer-swiller. They received a polite clap from their opponents. Trainset never did understand why fielders did that, when thirty seconds later they'd be trying to knock the batsmen's heads off. But Barmfield always followed protocol. 'Typical of cricket,' the Fixture Secretary cogitated.

Nutter mind-bogglingly did put one or two on the track. In fact he more or less won the match single-handedly. Figures of 7 for 29 were a bit generous, though. Two dubious lbw's were given by Biased Bob, both deliveries appearing to pitch nearer to square leg than to the stumps. And Bill caught one in the slips, an event which only usually happened when he wasn't wearing his wig, for some unclear reason. Well, to say that Bill caught it is a bit of an exaggeration, to be honest. It hit him somewhere on his chest, bounced off his shoulder, and then amazingly rolled back down the Skipper's arm and into his trouser pocket. All this whilst Bill was looking towards the heavens, in a futile attempt to pick out a big red cricket ball in a clear blue sky. So Trainset reckoned that a bowling analysis of 4 for 29 was, all things considered, a truer reflection of Nutter's abilities that day. But still, a 98 run win was mightily good. And Horrible Ugly Opener got a duck, which pleased Trainset no end.

So it was off to The Noseblower for a quick one. Or a slightly slower five. Apart from Vic, who'd moved much faster than he usually did, in taking his junior offspring home before they heard anything else that they shouldn't. And, of course, Omar, who'd gone to A&E for an X-Ray. Fortunately for the rest of the team, Persil had surprisingly condescended to join the limping Kenyan.

It was a good night. Biased Bob promised never to bring his sheepdog again, Mick said that he'd wash all of the genital protectors in strong bleach, and Bill finally admitted that his 'brilliant diving catch' had essentially been a bit of a fluke. Trainset vowed to calm down, and to phone Omar. In particular, Nutter was in fine form, telling all sorts of stories about effluent drains and their contents. He had his audience laughing hysterically. The trouble was that Nutter thought that they were all laughing with him, while Trainset was pretty sure that most of them were, in truth, laughing at him.

Barmfield must now have been about third in the table, and a good day had been had by all. Except for 'That scatter-brained cuckoo Omar'.

Steve grimaced. It was now time for the Sexy Sam story to be made public. And that could cause a few problems all round. He'd seriously considered writing a totally different account of the sixth game of the season, something much less embarrassing for all concerned. But in the end Steve felt that his classic masterpiece would lose a lot without the Sexy Sam bit. And he knew that Ted Carruthers wanted a bit of sex somewhere in his story. So he gritted his teeth and carried on...

CHAPTER SEVEN
MATCH SIX

I WANT TO HOLD YOUR HAND

Samantha Smith was Dave Jones' girlfriend. She and Dave lived together, and to everyone at the club they appeared the perfect couple. In many ways, each of them was almost too good to be true. Dave had a vivacious personality; Samantha's was off the Richter scale. And both were good-looking people, seemingly with the world at their feet.

Trainset was pretty sure that he wasn't the only one who thought that Samantha was a stunner. She was about five feet six, and had short brown hair, big brown eyes, and a superb figure. She was also very fashionable; if she wasn't in tight figure-hugging jeans, then she'd be almost wearing an immoderately short skirt. She smiled constantly, and was very jolly with everyone, whether they were male or female, Barmfield people or their opposition.

Samantha was known to them all as 'Sexy Sam.' Dave didn't appear to take any offence to either the nickname, or to her occasional flirting with other team members. This was doubtless because he was a quietly self-confident sort of guy, who just knew that she would always be 'his.' Sexy Sam was a legal secretary, at a solicitor's office in town.

Sexy Sam was a regular tea lady at home matches; at least she had been for the four years that Trainset had played for Barmfield. She always did a great job, nothing ever being too much trouble. In the last couple of years she'd sort of taken on the mantle of tea-manager, and she now organised the other tea ladies as well. Everyone was fully aware that she was more than capable of doing the whole lot herself, but other wives or girlfriends liked to come down to the ground, and none of the players wanted to put a stop such a healthy situation as that. This year Janet and Persil were Sexy Sam's assistants.

Sexy Sam didn't often travel to away games, so she'd clearly also got another life outside of Barmfield Cricket Club. But she was at this match, because Barmfield were at home, against Wollatown.

Today was to be the big game of the season. Whatever position either team held in the League was not of any great consequence. It was a local derby. The local derby of the year. Wollatown's ground was only about a mile up the road from Barmfield. Lots of the Barmfield players were friendly with others on the opposite side, to such an extent that it wasn't unknown for some of the Wollatown lads to join them in The Noseblower on a Saturday night. Cricket has a certain inter-club camaraderie, which is perhaps not so prevalent in other sports.

Omar had declared himself fit, following the previous week's problems. And Trainset had by now calmed down a bit. He was pleased that Omar was playing, assuming that he didn't repeat the brainless antics of seven days earlier, of course.

More surprisingly still, a bit of a crowd had turned up for the match. Looking out of the dressing room, Trainset could see perhaps twenty or thirty people sat in deckchairs around the boundary. Although their average age was about 87, and most of them would no doubt be dozing off in the near future, it was still good to start a game with people watching it. There was also a chap with a camera and tripod, who must have been from the press. The atmosphere was most definitely building nicely.

Bill won the toss and returned to the dressing room, telling his team, to their dismay, that he'd decided to field first.

'What have you done that for, Bill?' queried Des, aggressively. He went on. 'We won't win batting second. They've got good bowlers at the death, like Dave Trout and Joe Ling.' Moaner then chipped in. 'That's the first time I've ever heard Des talk sense. No doubt it'll be the last. But he's right, for once, Bill. You've made a naff awful decision. A complete howler, in fact.'

Before Bill could reply, Vic drifted into the changing room. He was late, yet again. Bill stared at Vic, then up at the heavens, shaking his head as he did so. A few giggled, including Trainset.

Bill then turned to Des, rather exasperatedly, 'Shut up Des. You may be an encyclopaedia regarding the Laws of Cricket, but I'm the Captain. I'm fielding first for a reason. Stop whittling on about those pipsqueak fish brothers, and concentrate on what we've got ourselves. We know Wollatown very well, so I reckon that we might give them a bit too much respect if we bat first. And in doing so, might not score enough runs. But if we bat second, and are forced into having to 'go for it' later on, I think that we've got the armoury in our batting line-up to win. And while I'm about it, I don't want any more of last week's fiasco from you, Omar. Can you please concentrate on the ruddy match today, rather than on your stupid prat of a missus? And you can shut up as well, Moaner.'

Des and Moaner quietly seethed, but said no more. Vic got changed, items of clothing flying in all directions as he did so. Trainset tried not to giggle again.

Wollatown batted very well. Despite still being 'not quite

100%,' Omar was the pick of the bowlers, picking up a 'five for.' Dave also got a few wickets. But Joe Ling's younger brother, Mick, scored 91 for Wollatown, coming in at Number Six. He hit it all over the place, losing three balls in the process. Luckily Biased Bob gave him out when he clearly wasn't, otherwise they'd have scored a lot more than they did. Still, 221 for five was a very good score. Barmfield now had a mountain to climb to win the match, and they'd somehow got to defuse another potential Biased Bob 'situation' as well.

Cricket-wise, things were not looking good as Barmfield took tea.

But Sexy Sam was looking stunningly good, particularly to Trainset. She was looking absolutely gorgeous. So much so that he couldn't concentrate on his food, which was very unusual for the Plumber. Sexy Sam had now developed what appeared to be an all-over tan, and was also wearing quite a lot of makeup. Her skirt, as usual, didn't leave much to the imagination. At one point she noticed that the Opening Bat wasn't eating much, so she asked 'Would you like anything else, instead, Trainset?' He somehow managed to refrain from answering that one.

Des and Trainset took to the field. Des was still carrying on about Bill's decision to bat first, but his partner was determined not to get involved in that argument. As they approached the wicket, Trainset heard some sort of commotion behind him, but thought no more of it.

The two openers got the innings off to a good start. They'd soon rattled up fifty odd, so the Wollatown Skipper decided to bring on Dave Trout with his off spin. All sorts of things seemed to be happening down at the Pavilion, but Trainset continued to try to blank out the noise. He was more interested in trying to hit Trouty over his head, and over the boundary.

Second ball he went for it. He hit it well. 'That's six pennyworth,' he said to himself, hardly bothering to run. It was a good hit, and it would have been six anywhere else on the ground. But the boundary at long off just happened to be a bit longer than elsewhere and Wollatown's 'new young lad' took a blinding one-handed running catch.

The Fixture Secretary trooped off, past Des, who was not happy. 'You moronic idiot, Trainset. That could have cost us the match. When will you ever learn?' he commented, in his usual straight to the point, somewhat uncomplimentary, style.

The Plumber got to the Pavilion. He was immediately collared by Dave.

'Sam's cut her finger. Quite badly. There's blood everywhere. Bill doesn't want any of our batsmen to leave, if he can avoid it. So we've been waiting for either you or Des to get out. You've finished your game now, Trainset, so could take her to hospital, please? If you don't want to go, I'll have to take her myself, and we'll just have to bat with ten. But Bill won't be happy if I do that. He'd appreciate it if you could take her, Trainset.'

There was no way that the Fixture Secretary wasn't going to take Sexy Sam to the local Accident & Emergency Department. He'd take her to the moon, if he could. But he didn't want to appear too keen.

'OK, Dave, I'll take her, if I must. Give me five minutes to get changed.'

Trainset got changed as fast as he'd ever done. He also concentrated on trying to make himself attractive to the opposite sex. Which wasn't easy. Ordinarily he wouldn't have overly bothered with the smelly side of things, as several of the other team members would no doubt concur. But today it was for Sexy Sam. So he showered, and plastered various important bits in antiperspirant, which he'd luckily found in Bill's bag. There was also a bit of after-shave in there, as well, which he reckoned that Bill wouldn't miss. He brushed his hair. He even practiced looking butch in the mirror, but gave that one up as a bit of a bad job.

Within six or seven minutes, he was outside with Dave and Sexy Sam. Trying desperately not to stand downwind of Dave.

Another couple of minutes and they were off. As they drove out of the car park Trainset could see Des on his way back to the Pavilion. Barmfield were sixty-five for two. It must have been about six o'clock.

Sexy Sam sat in the front passenger seat. Her left hand was covered in the biggest bandage that the Number Two Batsman had ever seen. She was a bit shaky. 'Thanks, Trainset. I'm sorry to put you out like this,' she said.

'No problem, Sam,' he said, glancing down at her beautiful long brown legs, which were hardly covered at all by her tiny little skirt. 'No problem at all.'

They got to the hospital. Sexy Sam's fear had made her somewhat unsteady. As they crossed the car park she clutched hold of the Plumber's arm. 'I want to hold your hand, Trainset,' she said. 'I'm feeling a bit funny.'

So, by the time that they got into the Department she was, unbelievably, holding Trainset's sweaty palm. With her right hand, of course.

Unusually, there weren't many people in A&E. They'd just beaten the Saturday night rush. So they were soon out again. Miss Perfect In Every Way seemed much happier now, as they got back into the car. She'd had six stitches, and some sort of injection, and been told to go home and take it easy for the evening.

'Remind me where you live, Sam,' said the chauffeur. He knew her address to the nearest inch, but he didn't want such a fact to be common knowledge.

'I'll direct you, it's not far.' They drove out of the hospital car park. Sexy Sam said 'You smell nice, Trainset. Is it a new after-shave or something?'

'It's nothing special. It's only my usual stuff, Sam,' he lied through his teeth. She went on 'It smells a lot like Dave's. I think it might be the same.'

The Fixture Secretary took stock of events, eventually realising his error. He thought. 'Shit. It wasn't Bill's bag. It was Dave's.'

As they drove on she looked at her injury. 'It's absolutely throbbing now, I think the blood's all rushing into it,' she said, rather forlornly. Somehow Trainset had this sort of second sense that she was getting much more friendly towards him.

So he didn't feel that he was being overly brave when he replied, 'I've got the same problem Sam. But mine's not my finger.'

If she hadn't laughed then, he'd have felt a right prat. But somehow he just knew that she would. She giggled and the spoke. 'We can't do much about my problem, Trainset. But when we get home I think that I might be able to help you with yours.' And with that, she put her good hand on his thigh. Mr Perky aroused further from his slumbers.

Barmfield's new version of Adonis couldn't believe what was happening. He'd never been very good with females. Yet, here was one of the best-looking women that he'd ever met, one he'd fantasised about for years, and one that he'd always thought was way out of his league, coming on strongly to him. Amazing!

It would have been about 7 o'clock by now, perhaps a bit later. Before they arrived at the house, he had thought of a few minor reservations. Well, in truth, about fifty major reservations. He wanted to mention some of them, but didn't know how to phrase things.

But Sexy Sam had read his mind. 'Don't worry, Trainset. I don't fancy you just because I'm full of drugs. I'm not on a high, or anything like that. I'm perfectly sane and rational. And I'm not going to leave Dave. And before you ask the next question, the answer is 'No – I haven't done this before with anybody else. I just like you Trainset; end of story. I don't suppose I'll ever do this again. It's probably my last fling before I marry Dave. Does that solve all your problems, Trainset?'

It certainly solved most of them. The only stumbling block now was that he felt very much a Barmfield player, and he knew that Dave did as well. They played together and drank together, and you don't usually let your team-mates down, do you? But he really, really fancied Sam. Fancied her rotten.

She got to the front door and Adonis Mark Two followed her in. It wasn't long before things moved forward. 'I need to nip to the loo, and also to have a quick wash. But I'm struggling to undress myself with this left hand being injured.

Can you help him take my clothes off, please, Trainset?'

He began to oblige. Shaking with excitement as he did so. He'd got as far as three and a half buttons on her blouse when disaster struck. The doorbell rang.

'Shit' said Miss Absolutely Gorgeous. 'It'll be Dave's Mum, I expect. She said that she'd most likely call round on her way home from the ground. She'll have come on the bus. I'd forgotten all about it. I'll have to let her in. Sorry, Trainset.'

The Plumber, not for the first time in his life, ran upstairs towards the Bathroom. But this time he was hiding from a potential disaster, as opposed to the more regular excuse of pretending to be working on something important. As he looked back from the Landing, he noticed that Sexy Sam was proving to be perfectly capable of fastening her blouse buttons with just one hand, after all. She boisterously opened the front door, at precisely the same time as Trainset surreptitiously closed his. He heard 'Come in Janet,' from his secret hideout.

The next problem then hit Trainset. He realised that Janet would have seen his car outside. 'That's torn it,' he muttered. There was nothing else for it; he would have to front it out. But he still had the potential catastrophe of Mr Perky impersonating a flagpole. Not that he was overly well endowed of course; but Sexy Sam had certainly brought out the best in him. There was no way Janet would miss the fact, especially as he was wearing his old jeans, which were at least two sizes too small. 'Ruddy typical,' he thought, wishing that he'd now never said 'Yes' to the damned hospital farce in the first place.

The Fixture Secretary could hear the conversation continuing downstairs. Sexy Sam was also clearly thinking on her feet. 'Trainset's been very good. We've just got home. He's nipped to the Bathroom.'

Upstairs, Lothario was beginning to panic. He needed to cool his nether regions down, ASAP. He saw the shower hose connected to the bath tap, and he started to use the facilities. Mr Perky slowly retired into minor mode. In his case, 'miniscule mode' would probably have been a more apt description. 'Thank God,' he sighed.

Before leaving the Bathroom, he remembered to pull the chain. Just for effect of course. With Mr Perky having been in the state that he had been, Trainset wouldn't have been capable of using the loo, in any case.

He went downstairs, and said his goodbyes to both of them. He headed for the front door. As he walked out, he vaguely heard Janet say something along the lines of 'Is he OK? I think he's urinated on his trousers, Sam. Did you notice?' The Fixture Secretary glanced down. He had clearly been slightly over zealous with the 'Mr Perky cooling down' process. The front of his jeans was saturated. 'Damn,' he thought. 'Damn, damn, damn and bugger it, bugger it, bugger it.'

Ten minutes later Adonis pulled into the Barmfield car park, just in time to see the two teams walking off the field. The bloke with the camera was snapping away merrily. Still sitting in his car, Trainset tried to suss out which team had been victorious. The scoreboard didn't help, as Young Tim was already taking the numbers down. Then he spotted Dave walking off with Mick. That was a great sight for the returning antihero. The Number Two Batsman shouted out to the rest of his non-existent passengers. 'We must have won. We've beaten Wollatown. Brilliant. Ruddy brilliant.'

Trainset shut his car door and hurried down to Stalag 9. Dave veered across towards him. They spoke simultaneously, answering each other's question as they did so. One reply was 'She's fine Dave. Just taking it easy at home. She's quite tired, though. Your Mum's there now'; the other was 'We won. Just, with one over left. It was a great game. And I got 66 not out.'

Dave then asked his team-mate a question that the recipient had hoped he wouldn't receive. 'Why are you wearing your cricket trousers, Trainset? You got changed before you left here.'

Lothario Number Two was proud of his off the cuff response. 'Sam was waving her hand about in the car, and my jeans got a bit spattered in blood.'

Dave said 'Oh, sorry about that. I'll pay for any cleaning costs. In fact I should buy you a new pair of jeans. I appreciate everything that you've done for us today, Trainset. Thanks very much. Oh, by the way, you didn't tip my bag over when you were getting changed, did you? My after-shave bottle has broken, and all my kit is stinking a bit now. It doesn't matter if you did, I just wondered how it had happened, that's all.'

The Fixture Secretary put on his innocent face. 'No Dave, not me.' He elected to say no more.

Dave went straight home. Trainset didn't stay long at the pub, either. After the day's events, he was a bit concerned that he'd get drunk and then go on to blurt something out to his mate Omar. And he could also see the 'What are we going to do about Biased Bob?' conversation coming up later in the evening. Especially with the Wollatown lads being there, apparently ready to pounce on the beleaguered Barmfield umpire. So he made some excuse about 'feeling a bit off,' and drove home. It had been a funny day. On the one hand he was so excited that he'd nearly got off with Sexy Sam. On the other he was honestly pleased for Dave that he hadn't.

They had beaten Wollatown, and they were third.

Trainset was getting ready for bed, whilst reviewing the day's rather exciting happenings. Suddenly something rather important crossed his mind. Had he turned the shower hose off? Or was the Jones's Bathroom now a reproduction of Niagara Falls on a bad day?

The Fixture Secretary decided to hope for the best. With a slightly furrowed brow, he got into bed, and within seconds was fast asleep.

'Thank God that's over with. Although I'm still a bit worried about what my Whingebag Wife might say when she reads it. Mind you, she hates me so much, she probably never will. And at least that fat Newspaper bloke will like the sex side of it'.

Steve was now so wrapped up in his memoirs that he'd even forgotten about the booze. A night without lager hadn't happened since he'd downed three cups of faeces-infected tea at Mrs Taylor's, and had ended up with gastroenteritis. Match Seven beckoned, and the scorebook highlighted one name that day…

CHAPTER EIGHT
MATCH SEVEN

IT'S NOW OR NEVER

Chris Boyce was known as 'Tantrum.' At 16, he was Barmfield's youngest player. He was also the loudest. Because he had been good enough to start playing senior Club cricket at the age of 13, he had moved well ahead of his schoolboy peers. The effect of this was that he had become, to say the least, somewhat big-headed about his abilities.

Trainset and the others felt that technically Tantrum had the quality to go right up to County level, but that his problems weren't ability-related. He'd never get any further than Barmfield CC unless he sorted his brain out. In fact, the way things were going, he might not be in their team for much longer. Tantrum didn't need a cricket coach; he needed a psychiatrist.

Several at the Club were also unimpressed by the fact that he spent his winter Saturday afternoons acting as Number

One yobbo supporter at the local professional Football Club. He'd already been arrested on three occasions for unruly behaviour, and no doubt worse was yet to come.

In looks, Tantrum was a bit like a junior Des. He was thick set, with blond hair. He wasn't particularly tall, but he had a strong, muscular physique. He looked quite a hard case, despite being still of tender years.

Trainset had this theory that underneath Tantrum's hardened exterior lay a heart of gold. But not many agreed, and, to tell the truth, the Fixture Secretary could see why. Des was always particularly scathing of Tantrum's attitude.

Barmfield had won four games on the trot. Things were going very well. Today they were away at Marby St Christopher's. Marby were a young club, who had started out about ten years ago, as a very low standard church team. But they had rapidly grown in stature, once they'd decided to open their doors to anyone, whether they were parishioners or not. So now they were quite similar to Barmfield in many ways. They had several very high quality players, but had still managed to hold on to a few of the original 'play for fun' members. Marby were therefore a mixed-bag sort of outfit, very much like Barmfield.

Trainset was pleased that his team were away this week. It meant that neither Janet nor Sexy Sam would be in attendance, and this was a great relief in the circumstances. He'd got another seven days for last week's highly embarrassing events to fade further into the distant past. Even better, he'd heard no mention of flooded Bathrooms, either.

Because Marby was a fair distance away, the Barmfield team had decided to meet at their home ground, and to travel in three cars. Trainset had been forewarned not to bring his van, but his 'car'. Ten of the players were there punctually; Vic again wasn't.

It was decided that Trainset should take his 'vehicle', his passengers being Tantrum, Hypo and Nutter. Similarly Des would also drive, complete with Biased Bob, Mick, Dave and young Tim. Because Bill was the most maniacal driver, and also had the fastest car, it was agreed that he would wait for Vic to turn up, and then take him, Moaner and Omar. Persil wasn't attending today, which was a huge comfort to all of the players, particularly Omar.

It had been observed that Bill was again sporting a full head of hair. So when Trainset's somewhat decrepit excuse for a vehicle had finally hobbled out of the Barmfield car Park, Tantrum and Hypo moved into in wig-appraisal mode. 'Do you think he sleeps in it?' queried Tantrum. Hypo replied. 'Of course he does. He's only bought it to spice up his sex life a bit. Ten to one Anne won't go near him when he hasn't got it on. I reckon he looks like some sort of weirdo without it.' They all laughed heartily. 'Mind you, thinking about it, he does with it on, as well,' Hypo added, to yet more raucous approval.

The conversation then changed to slightly more serious matters. 'I'm fed up with Vic being late every week,' said Tantrum 'You lot always criticise me for my behaviour. But I'm always punctual. I've never been late, in three years. Apart from the odd day when I've had to attend the cop shop for a Saturday morning rollicking.'

Trainset's attempt at a car arrived at the Marby ground. Des soon followed it into the car park. Both drivers had got a bit lost en route, so time was now of the essence. They made their way to the changing rooms. The opposition were already practicing in the nets. It was now 2.30pm, and the starting time was 2.45pm. To make matters worse, there was still no sign of Bill.

Barmfield had only got seven players, and they would have to start soon. They frantically discussed their problem. One suggestion was that Biased Bob would play, instead of doing the umpiring. In principle, this was a good idea, as it would at least have made them eight strong, and he had regularly opened the batting for years on end, albeit about a hundred years previous. But the Marby Skipper would have none of it, arguing that it wasn't fair on his own umpire. The Barmfield guys couldn't argue with this; being realistic, they'd have probably said the same themselves.

There was then another discussion as to whether Young Tim should play. Had Des been in Bill's car, Young Tim would definitely have been in the team. The others would have made sure of that, before Des arrived and had the chance to argue about it. But Des was there, and he yet again made it perfectly clear that he didn't want his fourteen-year-old son playing against quick bowling. The Plumber felt that Des was being overprotective, particularly as Tantrum had started at an earlier age. But Des hadn't yet reached a mature attitude on the subject. He wasn't prepared to even discuss the point. So neither did anyone else.

It was therefore back to seven again, with a batting line up of Des, Trainset, Tantrum, Dave, Hypo, Mick and Nutter. Looking on the bright side, if Bill never turned up at all, at least four of them were good bowlers. But, being more realistic, they'd have to be the best bowlers in the world, if they were to stand a chance of winning with only seven of them on the field.

'We can't wait any longer. Under the Rules of Cricket, we shouldn't really be starting at all with only seven players. But both teams still want to play. And we'll get fined if we start late. Or, even worse, we'll get points deducted. I'd better toss up,' said Des.

The seven of them were agreed, desperately hoping that Des would win the toss, and that Bill would turn up later. Fielding with seven men wouldn't be any fun at all; they'd be bound to lose in that situation.

Des walked out to the wicket with the Marby Skipper. He called correctly, much to the relief of the other six. Des and Trainset padded up.

As the two openers went out to bat, Tantrum and Dave were also getting prepared. It was a good job they did, as neither des nor Trainset lasted overly long. It was eight for two, and with only seven men in total. What a nightmare! Back on the pavilion steps, Des stared into the big blue yonder. 'Where the hell is Bill?' he implored of the Big Good Bloke Up There Somewhere.

Tantrum and Dave were at the wicket. They moved things

on to about twenty-five, and the scoreboard was starting to look slightly rosier.

Then it all kicked off. It was the most startling display of bad temper that Trainset had personally ever witnessed on a cricket field. Tantrum was given out, caught behind. The youngster was absolutely furious. They could all hear the screaming abuse, even from inside the Pavilion.

'I didn't hit it, umpire. You know that I didn't. You're a cheating idiot. You did this to me last year, as well. You're not fit to be standing there. I'll wrap this bat round your stupid head in a minute.'

Dave intervened, putting himself between Tantrum and the Marby umpire. There couldn't have been a better bloke to have out there than Dave. He was a very relaxed and popular guy, as well as being richly experienced. If Tantrum had been batting with say, Moaner or Nutter, it would have been all hell let loose. But it was still all pretty appalling, even with Dave trying to smooth things over. Tantrum wouldn't shut up, and was trying to push past Dave.

'Turn down that appeal, or you'll wish that you hadn't been born. I'm going to have you, you cheating idiot.'

Dave grabbed hold of Tantrum, and Des and Trainset ran onto the pitch to help him do so. Between the three of them they started to drag the now purple-faced Tantrum off the ground. Just as they were doing so, Bill's Jag tore into the car park. Stone chippings flew in all directions, showering nearby vehicles.

Whilst trying to force Tantrum into submission, Trainset could now see Bill, Moaner and Omar running down to the Dressing Room. Behind them was Vic, looking as though he'd been dragged through a hedge backwards. Again. As usual, various bits of kit were falling from his bag as he jogged along, very much in fourth place.

They arrived at the Pavilion more or less simultaneously. Dave, Des and Trainset were struggling with Tantrum, who now appeared to be foaming at the mouth. Bill and his passengers were desperately removing jumpers, shirts and shoes as they made for the changing room. Bob had also decided to nip back 'For a quick piss'. So all nine of them were trying to get through the Pavilion door at the same time. Well, seven of them, as Vic was still the best part of a hundred yards behind, and Tantrum was trying to force himself in the opposite direction, towards the man in white who'd ruined his day. It was mayhem.

'What the hell's going on?' screamed Bill.

'We'll tell you later, Bill. Just get changed as quickly as you can, for Christ's sake,' said Des.

Dave went back out, this time to bat with Hypo. As Des and Trainset had finished their efforts for the day, they decided to keep Tantrum to themselves, so as not to disturb those who'd still got to bat. Tantrum had calmed down slightly, so the two opening batsmen didn't have to manhandle him too much, as they all headed for Trainset's 'car'. They got in, Des ensuring that he was sitting in the back adjacent Tantrum.

Des started first. 'That little episode could well have cost you your career with Barmfield.'

The Fixture Secretary followed with his own criticism. 'And it's probably cost us lots of points, as well. The League Committee are going to crucify us for this, Tantrum.'

Tantrum's reply wasn't exactly full of remorse. 'I don't care a toss what you two say. You are the worst two players in the team. Apart from Bill, of course. I'm miles better than either of you two idiots. You can say what you like. I've got no respect for either of you. The only guy that I'll ever listen to is Dave. He's got more ability than you two put together.'

The sixteen year old was starting to get wound up again. He tried to get out of the car, but Des stopped him. Trainset decided that he ought to get into the back as well, in an attempt to prevent Tantrum doing something yet more stupid. But as the Plumber opened the driver's door, he spotted that Dave was now also out, and was wandering over towards them. A quick glance at the scoreboard showed Trainset that it was 58 for 4. Omar and Moaner were at the wicket. The Plumber could therefore remain in the front seat, whilst Dave got into the back, on the other side of Tantrum.

Whereas Des and Trainset had been very aggressive with Tantrum, Dave's approach was noticeably different. He was very calm, and very sensible.

'Look, Tantrum. Your problem is that you seem to need to constantly keep proving yourself. Can't you see that doing that is causing you all sorts of hassle? Why don't you just relax and take things as they come? You don't have to prove that you're a good player to us, because we already know that you are. And I guess that the same thing goes on down at the football, in the winter. I bet you are forever trying to show how hard you are to your mates, aren't you?'

Tantrum nodded. Dave continued. 'A mature adult doesn't need to try to convince others of his hardness, or of his sporting abilities. A grown man will know his own strengths and weaknesses, anyway. And he'll try to help others get better as well, not just spend his life concentrating on how fantastically he performs himself. Cricket is a team game. Can't you see all this, Tantrum?'

Tantrum again nodded. The two Barmfield opening batsmen were witnessing that someone was at last getting somewhere with their unruly teenager. Trainset couldn't fail to see that this was very impressive stuff from Dave. Though he was still annoyed with the all-rounder for having such a brilliant girlfriend.

Dave carried on. 'Having ability isn't the most important thing. Des and Trainset are not the greatest cricketers in the world. But they both know that themselves. You don't have to tell them. What's more important is that they are good team players. They always do their best, and also try to help others along the way. Tantrum, will you promise to just listen to me for the rest of this season? If you say 'Yes' to that, I'll sort it all out with Bill. And I'll support you at the next League Disciplinary Meeting. I want you to stay under my wing for a while. I'll promise to look after you, if you promise to listen to me. Will you do that, Tantrum?'

Again, their teenager nodded. But on this occasion it was all a bit different. He'd now started crying. In fact, he was weeping uncontrollably.

Trainset didn't know where to look, partly because his eyes were starting to well up in sympathy. 'Sorry, I've got a fly in my eye,' gabbled the Plumber, pathetically.

But Tantrum's crying didn't stop Dave. 'This might sound crazy to Des and Trainset. But I think that what you need is more responsibility. Not less. I reckon that if you had a role within the Club, you'd grow up much quicker. Tantrum, I'm going to put it to the Committee that you are our new School Liaison Officer. I'll propose you, and hopefully one of Des or Trainset will second it. What I want you to do is to get more young cricketing talent from your school down to the nets. And when you're capable of doing that job, I then want you to start visiting other local schools on Barmfield's behalf, as well. I believe that you can do this, Tantrum. In fact, with so many of your school aged friends and peers knowing of your ability, I'm confident that you'll be very successful at it. I'd like you to do all this for me, Tantrum. Will you do it?'

Tantrum whimpered 'Yes, Dave, I'm sorry. I'd love to do it. I truly would.' He then looked at Des and Trainset, tears streaming down his face. 'Sorry, Trainset. Sorry, Des.'

Dave continued. 'Good. But it's now or never, Tantrum. If you don't do what I ask of you straight away, you can forget Barmfield. In fact, you can forget cricket, full stop.'

Tantrum just carried on crying. In fact he sobbed so much that day that he never returned to the action at all. Which was probably a good job, bearing in mind what had happened earlier. The rest of them just left him in the Plumber's 'car', to get on with it.

The match continued. Barmfield scored 143. Not a lot, but with some good bowling, they could still win.

Mick rolled back the years, and also rolled over Marby. He was superb, taking seven wickets. And Hypo kept brilliantly as usual. Barmfield won by 18 runs.

When the game was over, Dave dragged Des, Bill and Trainset to visit the Marby Skipper and umpire. They explained what had happened in the car, and apologised profusely for earlier events on the pitch.

Their umpire was slightly sympathetic, but still very upset.

'I tell you what,' he said. 'If your young lad writes to me to apologise, I'll forget the whole thing. But I want that letter to be sincere, not just any old crap. I'll know if he really means what he writes; I'm not stupid. I'm still not happy, but let's just put it down to growing up, shall we?'

In Trainset's eyes, Dave was absolutely superb that day. He was forced to admit to himself that Sexy Sam was a lucky girl, having a bloke like that. There was no way he was in the same league as Dave. But more important than any of Trainset's own feelings was that Tantrum could, at long last, be starting to get his brain into gear.

After beginning with seven men, and finishing with ten, Barmfield had still won. The only real fly in the ointment was the recurring problem of the ever-late Vic. But the winning run was now reaching epic proportions.

The Plumber was heading for the halfway stage. Seven games down, and nine to go. Grinning like a Cheshire cat, he carried on typing…

CHAPTER NINE
MATCH EIGHT

GOD ONLY KNOWS

It was now Barmfield's eighth League match out of sixteen. Following Tantrum's performance of the previous week, the last thing that Bill wanted this time was another umpiring debacle. Barmfield were now getting an unfortunate reputation for overstepping the mark in this respect. But, as always seemed to be the case when Bill desperately didn't want something to happen, it did.

Most teams have a tearaway fast bowler, and Patrick 'Nutter' O'Broughton was Barmfield's. He was about six feet two inches tall, and very slim, with a mop of unkempt reddish hair. He originated from over the water. He'd never said from exactly where, other than it was 'a small village around the Galway Bay area.' He usually went in last man, and occasionally hit big sixes. A year or two ago, he had been a bit of a tearaway on the pitch, but at 23 years old he was now starting to calm down a bit. However, he could still have his moments. Nutter was a right arm quickie, with a tendency to be somewhat erratic. But he was a match-winner on his day, no question about that.

Nutter had earned his nickname for some of the stupid statements that emanated from his lips over the years. Whilst he believed that he was called Nutter as a complimentary reflection of his aggressive fast bowling skills, the rest of the Barmfield lads knew that it was really because, in their view anyway, he was as thick as a plank.

As has already been mentioned, the others tended to laugh at their number eleven, rather than with him. This occasionally bothered Trainset. He was more than happy to take the mickey out of such as Bill, but doing the same to a bloke like Nutter felt slightly wrong, somehow. However, he tried to console himself with the fact that if Nutter was happy, and didn't understand where the rest of the team were coming from, was it really such a problem after all?

Nutter was a drain-clearer by trade, so the others tried not to get involved in conversations about his job too often, particularly over tea. However this was proving more and more difficult, because Nutter now realised that mentioning such topics could often prove to be to his advantage. He had a big appetite, and he had eventually clocked on that a lecture about effluent properties, presented at the correct time and at the correct volume, generally left much more food for sewage experts.

Nutter also didn't bother too much in the hygiene department. Most of the other players tended to sit on the far side of the changing room, as near as possible to the windows, and as far away as possible from their fast bowler. Trainset had a bit of a reputation for occasionally being a bit whiffy; Nutter had a lot of a reputation for always being a lot whiffy. Particularly if he'd turned up direct from a Saturday morning foul cesspit job.

Today's fixture was at Danton Over Stale. Barmfield had won six games out of seven, so they were all in good heart. They'd decided to make their own travel arrangements, partly as it wasn't far away, and partly to avoid Vic making numerous other people late. Not wishing to let Vic drive there just when he felt like it, Trainset had arranged to pick him up en route. The chauffeur wasn't overly surprised to find Vic waiting outside his house, because he had half expected that the fiasco of the previous week would have had some sort of effect. Even on Vic. So, remarkably, the clergyman was therefore not delaying everyone else.

It was another hot day. Vic and Trainset arrived at Danton, and they parked in the pub car park, next to Bill, who was just getting out of his Jag. The Skipper was wearing his wig, due to last week's win. On such a glorious June afternoon, it struck Trainset that Bill's head could be getting a bit warm later on. They said their hellos, Bill noting loudly, and with no little feeling, that it was the first occasion this season that Vic had been early.

As Vic and the Plumber strolled up the fields to the Danton Pavilion, they noted that Hypo was sneezing away merrily, and was clearly looking for sympathy from Omar and Mick. They could also see that Des appeared to be vociferously arguing with Moaner about something or other. 'Nothing changes much, does it Trainset?' said Vic, whilst inadvertently trampling straight through a newly laid steaming pile of cow manure.

Out of the corner of his eye, Trainset noticed that Dave and Tantrum were in deep conversation, as they circumnavigated the far side of the ground. They were so close to each other that they seemed to be chained together by some form of invisible handcuffs. 'That's better, Tantrum,' the Fixture Secretary muttered, 'Keep it up.'

The Barmfield players congregated outside the Pavilion. They were very early, so there was no immediate rush to get changed. Away from the ears of the opposition, they started a bit of a team talk, but they had to abandon it when Moaner started calling Des a cheat. Apparently Des's bowling action had been discussed earlier.

'Why don't you two grow up?' queried Bill, somewhat impatiently.

Trainset picked up on his Skipper's comment. It struck him that a bloke who only wore his toupee when his team had won the previous week had no great right to be implying that Des and Moaner were acting childishly. So he questioned Bill, after firstly making sure that most of the others were listening. 'Why did you say that you were wearing your hairpiece this week, Skip?' The remark took the sting out of things, and Des and Moaner started laughing again.

Barmfield batted first. So, being last man in, Nutter's day was going to take a long while to get started. The visitors notched up 225 for five, which was considered to be a more than reasonable effort. Trainset top scored with 51, and Dave got a quick 43 not out near the end. Bill was beaming at tea, partly because of the score, partly because he hadn't had to face the embarrassment of batting himself, and partly because he'd been sitting in the sun, with his toupee preventing normal head self-cooling processes. He looked like a cartoon character, something like a beetroot wearing a brown furry cap. Nutter, of course, had also not been required to bat.

Now the Barmfield innings was finished, it was over to Nutter and Co. to try to win them the match. Nutter was to bowl first, from the sweetcorn field end. The umpire there was the Danton guy; a fairly rotund elderly chap, with big, thick, glasses.

Nutter stormed in for his first ball. It flew past the outside edge and Hypo took the ball cleanly, sniffling away as he did so. 'Well bowled, Nutter,' snuffled the stumper. 'Keep it there.'

The Danton umpire returned Hypo's comments with some of his own. 'He can keep it there all evening, if he wants to, but he'll be bowling every ball himself if he does.' The umpire then turned to the scorers and signalled that Nutter's first delivery was a wide ball.

Trainset was standing next to Bill in the slips, so he heard Bill whisper to Hypo.

'Was that an authentic wide, Hypo?' asked Bill. Hypo replied in the negative. 'No way, Skip, it was nine inches outside the off stump, at most. It was a quality delivery. It might have looked wide when I took it, because it was moving away after it passed their batsman. By the way Bill, I feel a bit off at the moment. I might need a drink soon.'

Bill kept his mouth shut, as Nutter raced in again. It was a repeat performance, the ball pitching just outside off and then seaming away towards first slip. 'Wide ball,' called their umpire again, signalling to the scorers as he did so.

Nutter was now starting to get a bit rattled. Even though his brain would never attain maximum revs, there was nothing wrong with his eyesight. He spoke to the umpire, loudly enough so that everyone heard 'Are you sure, Ump? It was only just outside off, wasn't it?'

'I'll do the umpiring. You do the bowling' was the curt reply.

And so it went on. There were fifteen deliveries in the first over, of which Danton's Number One batsman only made contact with two. Despite trying to play at all fifteen. The score had reached nine runs, all of which were wides. Before everyone changed ends for the second over, Vice-Captain Des ran over to the slip cordon, to discuss what had happened.

Hypo informed Des that, in his opinion, only one of Nutter's deliveries had properly been a wide, and that one was only marginally so. Des wasn't impressed, with either the umpire or with Bill. 'I don't care who's right or who's wrong, Bill. But you can't leave Nutter on,' he said. 'Well, not bowling from that end you can't, anyway.'

Bill now faced a real dilemma. If he took Nutter off, it could be seen as though he considered that the umpire was correct, which would further rile up the mad Irishman. And if he left him on, the Danton score would, very likely, rocket away, out of any sort of control. He walked slowly up to the other end, deep in thought, with Hypo and Trainset alongside. As he did so, he veered off towards the home umpire, who was by now ambling towards his square leg position. Hypo and Trainset partly followed, ensuring that they kept about five yards distance from their Captain. Nutter was also heading in the same direction, breathing heavily after his fifteen-ball stint in the heat.

Bill started first. 'We reckon that there was only one wide in that over, umpire. And even that one was arguable. We are not happy with the other eight calls. Why are you calling wides to balls that are a few inches outside off stump?'

It was the expected, reply. 'In my opinion they were wides, end of story. I'm the umpire, and my decision stands, whether you like it or not. If you've got any complaints, write to the League Umpires Committee after the match. Now let's play on.'

Bill was fuming, and he didn't want to let sleeping dogs lie. Especially as Nutter was by now also standing next to him, looking imploringly at Bill for support.

However, Hypo had seen the flaw in Bill's argument. Out of earshot of either umpire, he quietly reminded Bill that Biased Bob also had a similar sort of reputation. 'I know that he's not quite as bad as this chap, but our own umpire isn't exactly perfect in every way, is he, Bill?' whispered Hypo. He carried on. 'You'll have to be careful if you contact the League. It might be that Barmfield end up losing out more than Danton do.'

While Nutter was nearby, Trainset had a quick word, suggesting that he'd be better off bowling from closer to the umpire, rather than from wide on the crease. He explained that such a move should at least mean that the ball would be starting from a straighter position in the first place. Being somewhat short in the brain cell department, Nutter didn't seem to understand a word of what the Fixture Secretary was talking about. But, this aside, Trainset was still of the opinion that his idea was at least worth a try; so he kept reminding Nutter about it, eventually shouting at the bowler's diminishing back as the tall red haired Irishman perspired his way down to long leg, cursing remorselessly as he went.

For ten Barmfieldians, things temporarily cooled down as they moved into their fielding positions for Omar's first over. But their eleventh fielder, Nutter, was looking distinctly un-cool. In fact he was now extremely hot and bothered.

Omar's over passed by without any great excitement, the batsmen each scoring a single. So it was by now eleven for no wicket, after two overs.

'Now,' Trainset enthused to himself. 'The fun's about to start.'

Because Des had previously taken no notice whatsoever of Bill's advice, the Skipper decided to return the compliment. Nutter was to again bowl from the sweetcorn end. As the strike bowler walked slowly back towards the boundary, to start his exaggeratedly long run up, one or two rather pointed comments flew around the fielders, at a sufficiently high volume for Danton's man-in-white to hear.

'Good luck, Nutter. We're playing against twelve this week,' shouted Omar. Bill followed this up with a rather un-Captain-like comment of 'Knock his stupid head off, Nutter, then it ruddy well can't be ruddy well wide.' Bill had conveniently missed the 'above shoulder high element' rule in his argument, but none of the fielders were too bothered about such technicalities. Well, other than Des, they weren't. The Vice-Skipper was mentally running through the pros and cons of Rule 42.6, Parts (a) and (b), of the Laws of Cricket. Anyway, Bill's comment went down particularly well with their Number One, who gave the Barmfield Captain a rather strange look, whilst further securing his batting helmet, and changing to a batting guard of six inches outside leg stump.

Whether Nutter had taken heed of his earlier advice, Trainset had no idea. Whether he'd even understood it, he had no idea either. All he did know was that Nutter took a much straighter run up. At one point he disappeared behind his tormentor completely, and for one worrying moment, Trainset thought that Nutter was just going to run in and absolutely flatten the poor umpire, without delivering the ball at all. Or bowl from around the wicket, by mistake. But at the last split-second, the bowler sort of twisted around Mr I Love Danton, and his right arm appeared, ball in hand.

It was a good delivery, on off stump. But the Number One played it well, pushing it out to the left hand of Vic, who was fielding at mid-off. Bearing in mind that Vic was not the most athletic of fielders, there appeared to be an easy single. At least to the Barmfield fielders there did, anyway. However, the Danton batsmen were not aware of Vic's athletic frailties, and there was one of those farcical 'Yes, No' interludes, with both openers ending up being stranded in mid pitch.

Vic eventually got hold of the ball, and, somewhat surprisingly, chose to hurl it towards the bowler's end, rather than at the ever-snuffling, but still marginally alert, Hypo. God only knows why Vic threw it in that direction, but he did. God being closer to Vic than the rest of them, he was, without doubt, the only one who really understood Vic's logic.

Nutter dived back in an attempt to catch Vic's return. Well, 'dived' is gilding the lily slightly. He sort of stumbled backwards with his arms flailing hopefully in the general direction of that stupid little red thing that was heading towards him. And in doing so, collided with his beloved friend, the white-coated bespectacled Leader Of The Danton CC Supporters Club. The ball missed both parties, and also the stumps, and flew out towards long on, bouncing at high speed over the boundary rope. The batsmen had by this time crossed, so Vic had stupidly given away five runs.

The score was now sixteen for none, after two overs and one ball, which was hardly the greatest of starts. But at that moment the Barmfield lads witnessed what could prove to be a silver lining appearing around their dark grey cloud.

Mr Umpire From Hell was lying underneath Nutter. The stumps were shattered. One of the bails appearing to be sticking out of Nutter's ear, the other lost in the umpire's nether regions. The fast bowler looked a rather ghastly sight, what with his shirt round his head, and his legs round the umpire's neck. But the more elderly of the two men was in a much worse state. He was rolling around on the ground, holding his arm. 'I think I've broken my wrist,' he screamed. He was clearly in a lot of pain. Everyone knew instantly that the blind fat biased old codger had certainly broken something.

The Danton Skipper was seething. He raced out on to the square, remonstrating with all and sundry. 'You lot are a complete and utter disgrace,' he screamed, 'You'll be thrown out of this League if I have anything to do with it.' Several of his team followed him on to the outfield, each of them reading the riot act to the nearest Barmfield player. It was noticeable to Trainset that only Des seemed to be holding his own in any of the arguments; he was no doubt quoting Rules and Sub-Rules to an unfortunate Danton counterpart.

Bill strolled purposefully towards the Danton Skipper, and retorted with his own tirade. 'As far as I'm concerned, that umpire deserves everything that he's got. But if you believe that Nutter did it deliberately, then you must be ruddy mad. For a start, he isn't bright enough to even think of some sort of plan in the first place, never mind then having the ability to go on and put it into some sort of action.'

Bill knew that Nutter wouldn't hear any of this, as he was still extricating body parts from various pieces of umpire and stump. So the Skipper had managed to explain his reasoning, without letting his quickie know that he was considered by all to be less than a full shilling.

The game was temporarily suspended by Biased Bob. Players from both teams sat down on various parts of the outfield, hurling tirades of insults at each other. It was by now a very hot evening, so abuse was best carried out from a sitting position. Mr Blind Fat Biased Old Codger With Broken Wrist was helped off to the Pavilion. Des wasn't one of the helpers; he was more preoccupied with making Rule notes on his handkerchief.

Biased Bob stated that the teams were to have a five-minute cooling-down period, and then both Captains were to meet him privately to discuss what had happened, in order to try to find a way forward. The Barmfield umpire then nipped off the field, in order to relieve himself, while he had the chance. On his return, he, Bill and the opposition Skipper had a ten-minute meeting outside the Pavilion. Bill then returned to the square, calling all of his players around him, in order to explain what had been discussed. 'OK. Their Skip now realises that Nutter didn't do it on purpose. But he's still not happy with Omar and me for shouting abuse at their umpire. Anyway, cutting a long story short, it's all calmed down a bit now, so we're starting again. Biased Bob is going to be at the bowler's end for every ball, and one of their guys will be at square leg. But we are now in a bad position, so we'll have to bowl especially well to stop them winning it. For Christ's sake, Nutter, don't do anything else, or we'll have a riot on their hands. And it would also help if you tried to stay awake, Vic.'

The game restarted with the score on sixteen for no wicket, after 2.1 overs.

Nutter came in for the second ball of the interrupted over. Bill was fielding at first slip; Trainset was at second. Again, it was another good delivery, pitching on off and moving away. The ball did, at last, take the outside edge of the bat, and it flew straight towards the Plumber's midriff. In that split second Trainset felt confident; the ball was going to end up safely in his sweaty palms, he just knew it. But Captain Bill had other ideas. For some obscure reason known only to him, he stuck out a right arm, and in doing so successfully managed to deflect the ball past the Fixture Secretary's right boot, and down to the boundary for another four.

That was the final straw for Nutter. He raced down the pitch, hurling abuse at the unfortunate slip fielder. 'You ruddy stupid idiot, Bill. That was going straight into Trainset's hands. Have you got a brain, or what?'

What Bill wanted to say in reply was 'Yes, I have got a brain, Nutter. But, as sure is eggs is eggs, you have not. In fact you're as thick as a docker's sandwich. That's why you keep bowling the same delivery over and over again. And why the score is now twenty for none, after only fourteen balls.'

But the Barmfield Skipper was sufficiently bright to say the right thing, at the right time. Which in this case, was absolutely nothing. Nutter resorted to kicking the ground in sheer frustration. Trainset thought that the fast bowler looked a bit like a Spanish bull waiting for the off.

Surprisingly, Barmfield went on to win. Nutter's line improved, and Omar also bowled well. Danton made a good fist of it, falling 16 runs short, at 209 all out. Omar took three wickets, as did Dave. By 8.30pm, the Barmfield guys were in a far better mood down at the village pub, especially when they heard on the bush telegraph that Brialsford had lost to Wollatown.

Bill had always been very good at smoothing things over; he'd have made a good politician. So, after hearing the Barmfield Skipper's well-practised excuses, his Danton counterpart rather generously decided not to take any action against his visitors. He also promised that he'd do all in his power to stop the Danton umpire from complaining. All was now well again.

The Barmfield lads left the Danton Chequers several pints later, and in very good heart. Before departing, Bill wrote a short 'Apologies, and best wishes for a speedy recovery' note, which was to be handed to the Danton umpire on his return from Casualty. Most of the Barmfield players signed it, but Nutter refused to do so.

It was halfway through the season, and they'd won six on the bounce. Could anyone stop them now?

'That's half the season done. I reckon my blockbuster is brilliant so far. Lardo Carruthers is bound to like it. And if he says that he doesn't, I'll smack him one'. Steve Smith's chest expanded yet further. Now Match Nine was to feature Janet Jones…

CHAPTER TEN
MATCH NINE

YOU'RE MY WORLD

Janet Jones was Biased Bob's wife, and Dave's Mum. In the past she had spent years as a cricket widow, keeping herself away from the limelight while Bob enjoyed his prowess as the leading player at Barmfield. In those days, Bob Jones had been one of the top local batsmen, his claim to fame being that he had been picked for the County Second Eleven a few times in his youth. But that was all a long time ago. Bob was 65 now, Janet a couple of years younger.

Since Biased Bob took up umpiring, the Barmfield players had started to see more of Janet, and in the last few years she had become one of the tea ladies. Janet was still quite attractive, but now it was in a more motherly sort of way. She had clearly been a good-looker in her youth. She was smallish, about five feet two or so, and had managed so far to retain her light brown hair and slim figure. As a character, she was very pleasant with everyone, but generally preferred to keep herself to herself, unless she was forced into a situation where she had to open up a bit.

Janet had always played second string to Bob, and she seemed to be very much the stay at home, do the cooking and cleaning, type of a person. Janet certainly didn't come across as someone who'd be any good whatsoever at a general knowledge quiz.

Barmfield were at home against Oxbrook. It was a wet day, so there had been the usual round of phone calls during the morning. The eventual decision was to turn up for a normal start, as the forecast was good for later in the afternoon, and because both clubs needed a positive result. Mick had got the square nicely covered, so the teams were in a position to play a reduced overs match, once the weather had relented.

By 2.45PM players from both sides were milling around the tearoom. Unless something happened to use up a bit of time, it was going to be a long frustrating wait. Then Des came up with this plan to have a pre-match quiz. Everyone was to participate, but the whole thing was to be on a fun only, low-key basis.

It seemed a good idea, so the home team started to organise things. Sexy Sam was voted to be the question-mistress, on the basis that she would hold attention spans longer than anyone else. Hypo found an old Trivial Pursuit box in the store cupboard, which apparently he'd donated to the Club several years before. The quiz was therefore to be called the 'Hypo Cup.' Trainset sorted out the chairs and tables, in order that everyone would be facing Sexy Sam. No one could find enough paper or pencils, so it was decided that it would be on a 'first raised hand gets the chance to answer' basis. And that the winner would simply be the one who got most answers correct.

Trainset happened to hear Dave quietly tell Sexy Sam not to sit down, or she'd be showing her knickers to the audience. 'Boring Dave's ruined it again,' he thought to himself, cursing the ex-Skipper.

They were ready to start. Trainset was chosen to be the scorer, firstly on the basis that he ought to at least be capable of not cocking up such a simple task, and secondly because he was unlikely to be in contention for the prize.

Sexy Sam stood at the front, leaning against the back of a chair. 'Right, first question,' she said. 'What is the capital of Botswana?' About half a dozen hands were slowly raised. 'You were first,' she said to one of the Oxbrook players. 'So what's your answer?'

The chap replied, positively. 'Kampala.'

'No, sorry, that's wrong. I think that you were next, Janet. What is the capital of Botswana?' In reply, Janet suggested, rather uncertainly 'Er, is it er, Gaborone?'

'Correct, one point to Janet!'

Several of the Barmfield contingent looked at each other, somewhat amazed. There they were, architects and accountants, etc., and yet they'd hardly ever heard of Botswana, never mind Gaborone. Biased Bob seemed the most taken aback of all of them. Trainset thought that the fact that Biased Bob's wife had got a brain had never crossed her husband's mind over the forty-year period that they'd known each other.

The quiz was taken in good spirit, and so there were a few intentionally amusing replies. Like the one about the origin of a Mickey Finn, to which Tantrum suggested Mrs Fork Senior, whilst she had been shark spotting. And there was another about Axminster rugs, which yet again brought Bill's hairpiece into the limelight. Even the visitors thoroughly enjoyed that one.

But more belly laughs came from the unintentional mistakes. Three of them stood out above the rest.

The first one was when Sexy Sam asked the question 'Who wrote 'Daffodils?'' Apparently the answer should have been Wordsworth, but Des steadfastly believed that Alan Titchmarsh was the author. It took the other competitors the best part of five minutes to convince him that he was wrong. He seemed to get more and more wound up about it; he was convinced that he had got the book at home. He went on to say that, if Sexy Sam didn't believe him, then he would go and fetch it. Trainset knew that Des was competitive, but he hadn't realised quite how much. He thought that Des was going to explode, and disappear off home in a paddy. Had the question been on Cricket Law, no one would have tried to argue with Trainset's pedantic opening partner. But it wasn't, so they did.

Another good one was when John Logie Baird became an Irish lock forward. The answer to this one, not unsurprisingly, came from Nutter. 'I can remember him playing for Galway,' said the fast bowler, in the vain hope that the rest of them would simply take his word for it.

However Trainset's personal favourite was the response to the question 'In which film did Luke swallow 50 eggs in an hour?' Not being a film buff, he'd no idea that the correct answer was 'Cool Hand Luke.' But even he knew that the Oxbrook umpire was wrong when he answered 'The Ten Commandments.' The old codger must have been 75 if he was a day, and was clearly past his sell by date. Although the Number Two Batsman thought this answer to be absolutely hilarious, he also secretly hoped that the rest of the Official's faculties weren't completely up the spout, particularly bearing in mind that they were just about to start an important match.

The quiz was very successful. Although Trainset was scoring, he was still allowed to participate. So he got the one right about the number of ballcocks in an average semi-detached property. And Bill surprised everyone with a good answer about the mating technique of snails; apparently he'd read up on the subject a few days previous, in his Encyclopaedia Britannica, for some obscure reason.

But it was Janet who repeatedly answered correctly. Over and over again she gave the right reply, even giving the correct details to one about downhill skiing slopes in Western Australia.

The quiz was enjoyed so much that it was a while before anyone noticed that, outside the pavilion, the sun was starting to appear. It was therefore cricket time. The participants quickly called proceedings to a halt and Trainset totted up the scores. Janet had won by a distance. She ended up with seventeen points, the next highest score being nine, by an Oxbrook guy.

Janet therefore won the 'Hypo Cup.' Bill presented her with her prize, yet another spare bottle of whisky that he'd 'found' in his car boot. After she had received it, Trainset couldn't help but hear Biased Bob repeatedly interrogating her about how she knew so many facts. Her husband was totally bemused that she'd even had the confidence to call out her answers, never mind that she'd also got most of them correct. But Janet was trying desperately not to talk about her abilities to her hubby, especially in front of so many people.

The entertainment had been great fun. Surprisingly to Trainset, he didn't come last. That honour went to Nutter, who scored minus three. On most questions the Irishman wasn't quick enough to raise his hand. And, on the few occasions that he did achieve this element of the process, he then either forgot what the question had been in the first place, or gave a completely irrelevant reply. In fact, on reflection, the Plumber considered the John Logie Baird reply to be Nutter's best attempt of the afternoon. The Fixture Secretary mused that it was a good job that the Government had not yet introduced annual IQ performance tests for fast bowlers. But, on the basis that the rest of the world seemed to be heading in such a direction, no doubt that time would soon come.

Before leaving for the fresh air, there were a few snide comments from one or two of the Oxbrook blokes. They weren't happy about the way things had gone. Their problem was fourfold: (a) the questions had been supplied by Barmfield CC, (b) the question mistress was the girlfriend of the ex-Captain of Barmfield CC, (c) the scorer was a Barmfield CC opening bat, and (d) the prize-winner was a Barmfield CC tea lady. But, as usual, Bill was on the ball. He was always quick on the uptake, and had already anticipated an Oxbrook critique. The Barmfield Skipper stood and pronounced his thoughts, very authoritatively, to the miserable Oxbrook moaners. 'It wasn't a Barmfield player that won. In fact, of the players themselves, Oxbrook did better than we did. If you lot had brought along a female with a brain, she may well have given Janet a run for her money. But you didn't, did you? The winner is Janet Jones. End of story, chaps.'

The Oxbrook whingers immediately backed off. They thanked Sexy Sam and Trainset for their efforts, and praised Janet on her 'very impressive' performance.

Sexy Sam then almost threw both teams out of the pavilion door, so that she could quickly crack on with preparing the food.

Unfortunately, though, Barmfield lost the match. Being a 15-overs-a-side game, it all became harum-scarum stuff. Barmfield batted first, and made 95, the visiting right arm medium pacer taking all six wickets to fall. Oxbrook knocked them off with an over to spare, their best quiz contestant carrying his bat for fifty odd. The only player on Barmfield's side to shine at all was Nutter, who was sent in early and hit three big sixes in his 23. Bill was not a happy man as his team disconsolately trooped off to drown their sorrows.

It didn't take long for the bar talk to turn to Janet's quiz expertise. Biased Bob was positively beaming at his wife being the centre of attention. Even taking her to The Noseblower in the first place was a bit unusual. Generally she would go home straight after the match, to leave Biased Bob to 'have a pint with his mates.' This time, however, he not only took his missus along, but he also went completely OTT when he got there. He bought the whole pub a round of drinks, which was rather surprising, as previously he'd never been known to even buy himself a pint. Well, according to legend, not since his wedding day he hadn't, anyway. For the players, talking about Janet's performance was infinitely better than discussing the fact that they had played like prats, and could now be back to fifth in the table again.

Biased Bob continuously asked Janet why she'd done so well. Half of the pub was avidly listening, but pretending not to be. Eventually, after so much pressure from her beloved, she felt forced to reply.

'Bob, I was the top girl at our junior school. My IQ at eleven years old was recorded at over 170. My teachers were tipping me to have an outstanding career. They thought that I might become a leading businesswoman, or a Cambridge Lecturer, or something similar. But my parents just couldn't afford to send me to The Grammar. It wasn't the fees, as I'd been awarded a scholarship. It was because Mum and Dad needed me out at work as soon as possible. So I had to go to the local Secondary Modern. From there I just ended up working on the factory floor at Smiths, which is where I met you. I didn't tell you all this when we met, because I thought that it might put you off me. And I suppose I've just been happy to keep my light under a bushel a bit since then. I often go to the library when you're at work. And I'm quite good at all those quiz programmes on the telly. I hope you're not mad with me, Bob.'

Biased Bob put his arms round his wife. 'You daft ha'porth,' he said. His eyes started to water. 'I'm going to put you forward for one of those TV quizzes. You're bound to win it. You are a clever little monkey, Janet. I'm really proud of you. You're my world, Janet.' Biased Bob then nipped off to the toilet, to try to wash away the tears from his face. And to have a quick jimmy riddle, of course.

No one had ever seen such a display of emotion from Biased Bob before. It was such intense stuff that most of the other Barmfield players were completely transfixed. Trainset and Omar hardly spoke at all for half an hour or so.

Barmfield desperately needed to win the following week. In the meantime their beloved umpire would no doubt be phoning ITV and the BBC.

The death of Whingeing Wendy's Dad caused an unfortunate break in proceedings. Steve had got on very well with Tom. In fact he'd got on well with most of his wife's relatives. It just seemed to be Whingeing Wendy herself that drove him around the bend. He loved his wife, of course. But somehow they seemed to be drifting apart, at an ever-increasing rate. However, the Plumber knew that Wendy and Tom had been very close, and that the old bloke's death was going to create huge holes in Wendy's heart and mind. He also instinctively knew that it was now the time to take more interest in, and be more sympathetic with, his wife. So he spent several evenings listening to her weeping away whilst babbling on about her childhood. When she occasionally gave him the chance to get a word in, he gobbled out a few nonsensical trivialities, such as 'Aaahh', 'Never mind', and 'At least he won't be in pain', etc., etc. In short, Steve Smith's book had to go onto the back burner for over a week and a half.

Once the funeral of Tom was over with, it was then Vic's turn for the hairdryer treatment…

CHAPTER ELEVEN
MATCH TEN

ASHES TO ASHES

The Reverend Peter Maughan was based at the local C of E Church. Aged 30, he wasn't much older than Trainset. So he was remarkably young to have reached his current status in life. For obvious reasons, Peter was known as 'Vic'.

Vic was about five feet ten inches tall, with a mop of unruly, slightly thinning, dark hair, and a rather roundish sort of face. Although not yet particularly large, Trainset often used to think that when Vic got a bit older he could well end up looking like Friar-Tuck. Which would be rather appropriate, given his calling.

Vic was a very genial sort of character, and fairly shy. And he was very conscious that he should never push religion at his Barmfield team-mates. In fact he very rarely mentioned the subject; he just seemed happy to be 'one of the lads.' None of the team felt even slightly inhibited by his presence, which Trainset considered to be a great compliment to the bloke.

Vic was a top class Number Five batsman. At least he was when he was alert and awake. Which wasn't that often. He was one of the great frustrations of their Club, because of his rather disorganised character, both in timekeeping and in appearance. Vic often turned up late, and half asleep. How good he could have been if he'd got himself a bit more organised, they'd never know. But in some ways his frailties were also part of his charm. Vic was married to Alice, and they had a couple of young sons.

Because Barmfield's league fixtures were always on Saturdays, Vic was a regular player. The Club also played occasional Sunday friendly games, but Vic unfortunately had to give those a miss, due to more pressing commitments.

It was now mid-season, and the Barmfield contingent was starting to genuinely believe that the team could win some silverware. They were at home, against Warkestone. It was one of those typical English summer days, with blue sky alternating between high clouds. It didn't look as though it would rain heavily, but there was definitely a possibility of a quick shower at some point.

The game was about to start, and, as was often the case, Vic had yet to arrive. Mick was the first to mention the fact. He was 'Extremely unhappy about Vic being late,' especially as he had been at the ground since 'Just before 9am'. And that was after he'd had 'A bit of a lie-in.' Normally he'd have been there at more like 7am, but he'd been out with Vic the evening before at some Church function, and they'd both 'Had a few beers.' What was particularly annoying to Mick was that they'd both left fairly early from the entertainment, in order that they'd be 'Fit and raring to go' the next day. And that it was now 2.45pm and there was still no sign of Vic.

'What the hell does he do on a Saturday morning?' queried groundsman Mick, rather non-biblically, to the changing room in general.

Bill was clearly in a quandary, but he couldn't delay things much longer. He had to go out and throw the coin up, whether he'd got eleven players, or ten. Not for the first time this season, he discussed, with a couple of the others, the possibility of bringing their scorer, Young Tim, into the team, as a last minute substitute. But eventually he decided that doing that would only generate World War Three with Des. Bill felt that waiting for Vic was by far the better option.

The Barmfield Skipper decided that a little time-wasting wouldn't go amiss. At least this is what he told Trainset a couple of minutes later. But the recipient of this information wasn't sure that Bill's first attempt at tossing the coin, which ended in him losing it down one of the stump holes, was ipso facto intentional. Either way, it didn't work, as the opposition Captain had been caught out like that before, and so carried pockets full of loose change to every tossing up performance. Bill's 'plan' therefore misfired. In any case, the Barmfield Skipper eventually did win the toss, which solved some of his problems. Despite the absent Vic being their regular Number Five, Bill decided to bat.

In these circumstances the last thing that Bill needed was to lose both of his openers early. Especially as Barmfield were now getting into some sort of winning run. But, as usually happens in these situations, that is exactly what he got. Des and Trainset only lasted a couple of overs between them. Warkestone had imported a West Indian left-armer this season, and he was good. It was five for two, and no sign of Vic.

Bill was getting his hair off. Which was a bit paradoxical, because, as Barmfield had lost to Oxbrook the week before, he was back to Kojak mode. Mr Axminster was nowhere to be seen. From inside Stalag 9, the Fixture Secretary could hear his Captain seething. 'I thought that men of the cloth were supposed to be responsible and thoughtful to others. Where is the stupid prat? And, talking about prats, I don't know why Trainset played that dog's dinner of a shot, either; I wish he'd listen to me more often. I don't think that he plays for the team at all. He's a selfish bugger. And he's always winding me up, as well.'

Omar and Moaner and were now at the crease, and

Trainset watched events from the changing room window. Barmfield were now 14 for two after six overs, and both batsmen were struggling to stay there. The whole team were desperate that Vic showed up, preferably before another wicket fell.

Moaner was hit on the pads. There was an enormous shout of 'Owzat' from most of the Warkestone team. They all held their breath. 'No Ball,' signalled the Warkestone umpire. There was a huge sigh of relief from the deckchairs.

Trainset decided to take a stroll around the ground. Des and Nutter joined him.

'What I can't understand,' said Des, 'Why someone with all that ability doesn't use it to the full. I'm no great cricketer, but I always try 100%, all game every game. I'm totally committed.'

Nutter picked up on the Vice-Captain's comment. 'Committed? I think you should be committed, Des. Committed to one of the local nuthouses.'

This was the first proper wisecrack that Trainset had heard from their opening bowler. Well, the first one that made any sense, at any rate. Not exactly a side-splitter, but for Nutter it was very good. Its contents were perhaps more appropriate to the teller, rather than the recipient. But they all laughed anyway, Des noticeably less enthusiastically than the other two.

The Barmfield threesome were by now getting more and more concerned about Vic. Des had undeniably hit the nail on the head. They were starting to become very annoyed indeed with their Number Five.

As the three of them approached their first circumnavigation of the ground, Vic's Godmobile chugged slowly into the car park. Smoke and steam were belching out in all directions and from every available orifice. What was left of the vehicle's engine appeared to be about to explode. A yet more bedraggled than usual Vic appeared, extricating himself from the stinking, pathetic pile of scrap metal. The driver was red-faced, and, even from a hundred yards away, the trio could see that Goddo was sweating profusely.

Des, Nutter and Trainset watched as Bill jumped up from his deckchair and raced towards the late arrival. As the bald-headed Skipper neared the current Most Hated Man On Earth, he frantically waved his arms around, and shouted extremely rude words at the Very Reverend Peter Maughan. They could hear the heated conversation from their distant viewpoint. 'Where the hell have you been, Vic? You're always effing ruddy well late. You're batting next, you moron. You stupid effing wally. Get effing changed.'

'I'll tell you about it later, Skip,' shouted Vic, barging past Bill in his haste to get to the relative sanctity of the changing room. Vic had his bat in one hand, his boots in another, and his kitbag under his arm. He was wearing his church outfit, complete with surplice, dog collar and all. Being somewhat nosey, Trainset left Des and Nutter, and rapidly jogged across towards the Skipper and the Number Five. As the two of them marched along the path towards the building, Trainset took up a position just behind. From here, he was in an ideal place, not only to pick up all of the conversation, but also to pick up various loose pieces of Vic's kit at the same time.

Bill and Vic entered the changing room. Trainset, not wishing to miss out on a bit of fun, was there within milliseconds. Bill started screaming again.

'You're never effing well on time, Vic, I'm getting effing fed up with it. It's just not effing fair on the rest of us.' He grabbed the assortment of filthy socks, towels and jockstraps from Trainset's arms, and threw them straight at Vic's scowling face. 'And you might need these effers as well. You dropped them all over the effing field. As effing usual.'

Bill stared at Vic, his eyes blazing with anger. Trainset temporarily assisted the situation by yet again picking up some of the foul smelling assortment of rubbish that Vic called his kit. Trainset was enjoying things, and he didn't want to diffuse the fun yet. So he asked Bill a rather pertinent question.

'Skip, didn't we make a rule last season that all players should turn out in clean, neat, equipment? I think we did it in order to generate a better team spirit, didn't we? And didn't we also say that anyone who didn't comply would have to pay a fine?'

Having stirred things up nicely, Trainset left Vic and the Skipper to discuss the Reverend's lack of sartorial elegance. Whilst receiving another extremely loud earbashing, Vic got changed, and sheepishly shuffled outside to join the rest of the team. He'd already got padded up, and was ready to bat. But he didn't exactly look the part. In fact, if anything, he looked even 'less the part' than he usually did. Which was really saying something. He was wearing old boots, with holes in the sides, and his shirt was not only filthy, but also ripped. And he'd forgotten to remove his dog collar, as well. In Trainset's eyes, Vic looked a complete and absolute arsehole.

The others were, by now, perched on the edges of their seats, preparing to give their Number Five a bit more earache. Particularly because this game, if played properly, could see them moving up towards the top of the League. But luck favoured Vic. Before the rest of them got a proper opportunity to open their mouths to discuss his latest misdemeanour, Moaner was given out, and the Reverend was off like a rocket, in order to avoid further recriminations.

Vic batted superbly, and was still there after the forty overs duration. Trainset thought that the probability of them all lacing into him, should he have returned to the pavilion, was just the spur that he needed to make him stay out there. He finished on 88 not out, in the Barmfield total of 157 for 8. Only Dave Jones gave him much help, and he undoubtedly struggled in making 21. The total score wasn't great, but at least Vic had given them a sniff of a chance.

It was noticeable that Reverend Vic maintained a certain distance for the remainder of the day. He opted out of tea, on the basis that he 'Needed some fresh air.' And he was very quiet in the field, as well. The weather had held off, after all. So, by the end of the match, which Barmfield won by 14 runs, Vic had managed to successfully avoid having to talk to anyone about why he was, yet again, late.

But as they headed off to get changed at the end of the game, he knew that now was the time to receive a lambasting from all and sundry.

Bill started first. 'It's just not good enough, Vic. Granted you've batted well, and you've won us the match. But that's not the point, Vic. This is a team game you know.'

Mick joined in. 'I was with you last night, Vic. You said you were going to have a good night's sleep so that you would be fine for today. I was down here by nine o'clock, and that's late for me. You are totally selfish and completely unreliable, Vic.'

Moaner went further. 'You aren't that good, anyway, in my opinion. We could easily find somebody better than you. You're a complete waste of space.'

Bill chastised Moaner. Then he had another go at Goddo. 'Vic, you've got a phone. So have I. Might I respectfully suggest that you make the superhuman effort of taking yours off the hook and pressing a few numbers? Or is even that too much effort?'

And so it went on. They absolutely crucified the poor bloke. But he didn't storm off home. He just listened to it all, every so often apologising profusely. It was clear that Vic wanted to say something, but the others were not in the mood to give him that chance. It must have been a good ten minutes before he finally managed to get a word in.

Vic's first attempt at explaining his lateness didn't help his cause.

'Sorry, Skip,' he said to Bill. 'On the way over, I needed some petrol, so I stopped at the supermarket down the road. I filled up, and went in to pay. I didn't take much notice how much it was; I just paid with my God Is Great Credit Card. It was only when I was leaving the kiosk that I looked at my receipt, and realised that I'd told the cashier the wrong pump number. My bill was over £200, because I'd paid for the double-decker bus in the next lane. But the bus had by then driven off, its driver having apparently paid my £15 bill. When I went back in to complain, they were adamant that I still had to pay the £200. In fact they seemed to think that I should pay the £15 bill, as well. God knows why. Er, sorry, God, I shouldn't have said that. Anyway, all that lot delayed me several minutes. And I think that I might have put diesel into the tank by mistake, because my car's playing up a bit now.'

'Stupid plonker,' said Moaner.

The story was obviously true, and typical of Vic. But Bill wanted to know more about the weekly problems, rather than today's specific ones. He was exasperated. 'For Christ's sake, Vic,' he said, somewhat unreligiously, to the local man of the cloth. 'Why don't you effing well wake up in the mornings, like the rest of us? That petrol fiasco only explains ten minutes or so. Or should I say diesel fiasco? Anyway, what's the real reason, Vic?'

Vic now felt that he had to come clean. 'OK. I had a big problem. One of my parishioners, Mrs Baker, died in the night, and I had to go round there at 4am and give her the last rites. Next week it'll be Ashes to Ashes, and all that. I think some of you knew her; she used to do the teas years ago. I tried to phone you at about 10 o'clock this morning, Bill, but you were out. I didn't leave a message, because I'd got no real idea of what message to leave. I didn't really know when I'd be able get here. I meant to try you again later, but it's all been a bit hectic. I've been with her family all morning. They are in a right state. And the reason that my kit is in a bit of a mess is that my missus is in hospital. She's having our third kid, and there are complications at the moment. I've got one of those new mobile phone things, but I've broken it already, and I've just not had time to sort it out. Sorry again, Skip. If you drop me for next week, I'll understand why.'

Moaner chimed in. 'I suppose that explains today. That's if we believe you, of course. Which I don't. But what about every other time that you've been late? Which is just about every ruddy week, by the way.'

Vic spoke again. 'Sorry, Moaner. I have had similar problems all season. My wife has had these birth complications for weeks. And there is often a call in the middle of the night from somebody or other. One of the problems is that vandals choose Friday nights to break into the Church. So I've been down there regularly at 3am on Saturday mornings with the police. And if it's not that, it's something else. As I said before, I've been struggling to get any sleep all summer.'

Vic finished off. 'To be fair, I think it's better if I jack it all in at the end of the season. I love playing cricket. And I think the world of you miserable lot of no-hopers. But I just cannot guarantee to be here on time. I really wish that I could, but I can't. I know that I'm a complete let-down. And I know that I'm always making problems for you, Bill. I just feel so guilty about it all. I don't know what else to say. If there were some way I could make it right with you all, I'd do it. Whatever it took, I'd do it. I'm just so sorry, chaps.'

Moaner didn't believe Vic, but the rest of them did. In about thirty seconds flat, nine blokes had totally changed in demeanour. Moaner didn't understand the words 'having feelings.'

The others had been aggressive, self-righteous, and downright self-opinionated towards Vic. Now, apart from Moaner, they were totally embarrassed, and many of them were more than upset. They all wished that they could rewind the day back to 2pm and start it again. They'd all thought the worse of Vic, for the whole of the afternoon. And they hadn't given him chance to explain. Now they just didn't know what to say to him.

Several of them just stood and watched Bill applying a few final layers of antiperspirant, and checking his 'hair' in the mirror. They saw Vic quietly leave. Then they shuffled out of the changing room, in ones and twos. They'd crucified poor Goddo. Trainset had tears in his eyes, and he noticed that one or two of the others had as well. Most of the players had known Mrs Baker, and they were very sorry to hear of her death. Several of the team had also met Vic's wife on occasions. But it was their treatment of one of their colleagues that had truly got to the more sensitive souls amongst them. They knew that, whatever they said to Vic from now on, they could never take back what they'd all just done to him. They were acutely aware that their relationship with him had changed forever. And that he most probably wouldn't play again next season.

'Shit,' Trainset muttered as he walked to his car. 'Shit, shit, shit.'

It was a very quiet night in The Noseblower, even though they'd won. Omar didn't say a lot, partly due to earlier events, and partly due to the fact that the horrible Persil was sitting next to him. Vic didn't show at all.

Bill seemed to think that Barmfield were now second. But no one particularly cared any more.

Making up for lost time, the Plumber moved straight on with Match Eleven. This one was a case of 'Tim Price, I hope that you never read this...'

CHAPTER TWELVE
MATCH ELEVEN

IT'S MY LIFE

Timothy Price was Des Price's son. Known as 'Young Tim,' he was rather quiet for a teenager, and he tended to only speak when he was spoken to. Trainset suspected that this reserve was due in no small measure to Tim's father being so blunt and aggressive. Des was quite old-fashioned in a lot of ways, particularly when it came to being very much the father figure within his family.

Young Tim was blond haired, and wore glasses. He was very slim, particularly in comparison with his father. He was also fairly tall, about six feet, perhaps a little more. The Fixture Secretary wasn't sure precisely at what age teenagers stop growing vertically, but Young Tim was surely now approaching that point. So Trainset guessed that Young Tim would 'fill out a bit' from now on, eventually ending up with more like his Dad's solid build. He could therefore become a very big strong bloke, with a good fast bowler physique.

Young Tim was now in the third year at the local secondary school. Apparently he played cricket for their under fourteen team, but Barmfield had not, at least up to now, witnessed his abilities. If they were playing at home, he tended to turn up with his Dad, do the scoring, and then make his own way home, immediately the game finished. If they were on their travels, Des would typically bring him to the match, and then afterwards drop him off somewhere near their house, on his own way to The Noseblower.

Young Tim had not, as yet, attended any club net practices. Des had said on numerous occasions that he was not keen on his son playing 'men's cricket,' until he was 'a bit older.' Most of the others thought that this was probably an error on Des's part, but, at the end of the day, they didn't know what had been discussed at the Price residence. For instance, it could be that Des really wanted his son to play, but Young Tim himself didn't fancy it. And in such a situation, Des could well then be telling others that his son wasn't 'old enough,' as some sort of cover to protect his son. In summary, the other players didn't understand why Young Tim hadn't shown any great appetite so far to join in, but this didn't stop them wanting him to.

Young Tim was clearly a bright lad; carrying out the scoring procedures was of no great difficulty to him. Often the opposition team would turn up scorer-less, and he would do the job on his own. Being interested in both maths and IT, he was somewhat boffin-like, and he had never been known to make a mistake.

Young Tim had not reached the girlfriend stage yet. In fact he didn't appear, on the face of it at least, to have many friends at all, male or female.

Today's game was at Brindon. The village wasn't far away, so the Barmfield guys were all 'travelling direct.' Brindon had a coal mining background, so neither the cricket field nor its environs were overly picturesque. And the opposition were perhaps more 'cloth cap' in character than most of the other sides in the League. The pit itself was now closed, but the villagers still had that 'hard worn look' about them. To be fair, Trainset considered the Brindon team to be great blokes under the surface. Under the surface in the sense of their character, not when they were half a mile underground. It was just that they were just much more rough and ready than the Plumber's own team-mates. The nearest that Brindon had in their team to an architect was the local butcher, and Trainset guessed that several of their side were, in all probability, on the dole.

Trainset personally didn't like playing at Brindon. Not because he felt that Barmfield were 'a better class' than the opposition; he certainly hoped that he was not that sort of person. It was more because the whole place just depressed him. He know that this attitude was selfish, and that it was precisely because of the visits of other sports teams like his that the villagers would hopefully start to pull themselves out of the doldrums. He had great sympathy for their social and financial problems. In fact he felt that he always got on well with a lot of their team. But he hated going there, nevertheless.

Barmfield were to bat first. As Des and Trainset began to prepare, Young Tim was already in the little scoring hut, sorting out his pencils, rubbers, sharpeners and scorebook. As Trainset got padded up, he glanced out of the window. He could see a pretty teenage girl, obviously the daughter of one of their opposition. He assumed that she was a spectator, or perhaps a tea girl. It wasn't until he emerged into the sunlight that he realised that she was by now also in the score-hut, sitting next to Young Tim.

This was going to be interesting, Trainset meditated, particularly as the nearest that Young Tim had been to this sort of situation before was if one of the adult tea ladies had sat next to him. How would young Tim cope with a little blond stunner of a similar age to himself?

Whilst waiting for the last couple of the opposition players to take to the field, Des and Trainset peered through the score-hut window, in order to introduce themselves to the girl.

The Fixture Secretary did so because he was intrigued, and because he felt that a little 'winding-up' wouldn't go amiss. And he was pretty sure that the Number One Batsman did so because of fatherly concern that his son was going to be smitten by some blond bombshell, and end up making her pregnant. This was a rather unlikely scenario, in Trainset's opinion. But the Number Two was convinced that it was where the Number One's brain processes were heading. Des and his accomplice at the top of the batting order were therefore at totally opposing ends of the spectrum in their reasons for introducing themselves to the young nymphet.

Des started. 'Hello. This is my son, Tim. He's fourteen. He's a very bright lad. He'll help you out, if you go wrong. I'm Des, and this is Trainset.'

It didn't take them long to suss out that the girl was a bit of a character, to say the least. Her reply was very pointed.

'Hello. My name is Claire, but my friends call me Blondie. I'm fourteen as well, but most people think I'm about sixteen, what with my long blond hair, and my big boobs. I have scored a few times before. And I've scored a few times in cricket scorebooks as well.'

Blondie giggled, seductively. Then carried on. 'I might make the odd mistake this afternoon, so I could need some help from Young Tim. He is very nice looking, isn't he? He's got lovely eyes, and a really nice bum. I think that he takes after his Dad. So, if he helps me with the scoring, I'll help him with anything else that he needs. Anything at all.'

Trainset couldn't see too well into the dimly lit score-box, but it looked as though Young Tim was by now bright red, sweating, and squirming about in his seat. But his Dad was in the sunlight, and it was blindingly apparent to all that he categorically was bright red, sweating and squirming about in his pads. The fact that he was covered from head to foot in three layers of protective equipment was not helping Des to keep his cool.

Trainset reckoned that Young Tim's natural instinct would normally have been to throw down his scoring kit, and to storm out of the score-hut and also out of the ground. But the

Plumber knew, and Young Tim knew, that there was nowhere to go. Had they have been playing at Barmfield, he could have just walked home. Had they have been playing at one of the other more picturesque away grounds, he could have gone off for a cooling-down stroll. But they were at Brindon, so the best that he would achieve in the village would be to obtain a stream of verbal abuse from the local yobbos. Young Tim was a bit stuffed. So he had to stick it out.

Trainset judged that Young Tim would stay, and would eventually get over his embarrassment. But that his Dad wouldn't get over his for a long, long while, because of his rather closed-minded attitude. This situation was absolutely brilliant, in the eyes of the Barmfield Fixture Secretary. He couldn't miss an opportunity to further wind up Des, particularly as Hypo and Omar had now joined them. So Trainset quickly beat his rather traditionally-minded colleague to the next question, putting things straight onto the same wavelength as Blondie.

'Young Tim is a very good scorer. But I'd like to see him start playing the game soon. You're the same age, so he might listen to you. Do you think that you could chat to him this afternoon, and try to encourage him to be a bit more daring from now on? Perhaps to put his pencils down and put his cricket kit on instead? Do you think that you could you encourage him to take a few more risks?'

Before Blondie could reply, Young Tim came out with what the questioner believed were the first words that the scorer had ever spoken to him. 'Get stuffed, Trainset. You shit-stirring moron.' He then turned towards his father. 'And you're as bad, Dad. Stop talking about me like I'm a mangy little two-year-old. It's my life, and I'll do what I want.'

Blondie carried on where she'd left off. 'Yes. I'll help him put his cricket kit on. Whenever he wants me to. Can I start with his box?' Hypo and Omar laughed hysterically.

Des and Trainset went out to bat, each having a distinctly different opinion of Miss Bombshell. 'Nice girl. Quite a lively character. Could be good for your Tim,' said the Fixture Secretary. 'Gormless little scrubber. It's typical of this shit hole of a place. I'll be glad when we can go home. It's all your stupid fault, Trainset,' was Des's abrupt response. Dexter Price's opening partner was still giggling as the Number One took guard.

Des and Trainset batted quite well. If Des was still a bit 'off' with his partner, he didn't show it. After eight overs, the scoreboard was showing forty-two for no wicket.

At the start of the next over, Trainset clipped a nice shot off his legs, for three. This was followed up two balls later by Des hammering one off the back foot behind square, to the boundary. So the Fixture Secretary calculated that they should now have been forty-nine. But the scoreboard was now only showing forty-one.

To start with, the two openers didn't bother too much. They just assumed that all would sort itself out. Neither of them was the sort of player that totted up his own score; both of them just relied on the scorers to do their job. And they both knew that Young Tim was very good at it. So they just concentrated on batting.

But, as the innings progressed, the scoreboard was becoming more and more erratic. One minute it was in the sixties, the next in the fifties. There were even numbers going up in the wickets column, when Des and Trainset were clearly still batting.

Eventually Des spoke to Biased Bob. 'Can we stop for a quick score check, please, umpire? We've got no idea where we are. There might be something wrong with the scoreboard.'

Biased Bob stopped play, and walked back to the Pavilion. Having firstly nipped in for a quick wee, he then went over to the score-box to talk to Young Tim and Blondie. He asked them to take an over to sort things out, and then to shout out the correct score, at the end of the next over. On Biased Bob's return to his square leg position, they were all told, in no uncertain terms, by the Brindon Skipper, that the problem was definitely not 'scoreboard-related,' but 'scorer-related.'

The next over came and went. But there now seemed to be yet more confusion. Des and Trainset could see that Bill,

Hypo and Nutter were all now with the two teenagers, obviously trying to help them sort out the mess. Quite what Nutter thought he could contribute to a mathematical conversation, the Fixture Secretary had little idea. But at least the fast bowler seemed to be trying to help.

Des was now not only annoyed because he had no idea of Barmfield's progress, but also because it was his own son who was seemingly generating the problems. At the end of the eleventh over, he also walked down towards the Pavilion, shouting to Young Tim as he approached. Trainset followed, a few yards behind.

'What in God's name is going on, Tim? Are we 56, or 67 or 73? We've had about every number between fifty and eighty-five on the board in the last ten minutes. How many runs have we ruddy well got, Tim?'

Tim didn't reply, but Bill did. 'Shut up Des. We are still trying to sort it all out. I think what's happened is that the two scorebooks have somehow got mixed up. It looks to me like Young Tim has been scoring in both books at the same time, but that Blondie has been also putting some runs down in the Brindon book. So the score in the Brindon book is currently nineteen more than in the Barmfield one. Not only that, but Young Tim seems to have given Trainset out caught behind, about four overs ago, for some obscure reason. It's all a complete cock up. You carry on batting, Des, and we'll try to clear things up.'

On the way back to the wicket, Trainset just couldn't stop laughing. In fact he was almost doubled up with hysterics. His stomach hurt. It was side-splitting stuff. Clearly Young Tim had got so besotted with Blondie in that rather dark, private, score-box, that he'd completely lost it. Blondie was not only rather suggestive in the talking department, but the Plumber suspected that she'd perhaps also been a bit suggestive in the physical side of things, as well. He wondered if this could be the first case of its kind in cricket history. He'd certainly not seen 'wandering female hands stopped play' in any of the sporting pages that he'd read.

By now most of the Barmfield team were there, trying to

sort out the mess. Trainset considered it all to be absolutely hilarious. Unusually for him, he wanted to get himself out, and get back down to the score-box as soon as possible, to join in the fun.

Des, on the other hand, was not quite so amused. In fact he was absolutely boiling. 'It's that mentally deficient girl's fault. Tim's fine on his own. She's ruddy deranged. And she's a cheap little tart, as well,' he screamed, at anyone who cared to listen.

The Brindon wicket-keeper heard Des's outburst. He responded at full volume, all guns blazing. 'That's my daughter that you're talking about. Shut your face, you stupid fat prat.'

For the Fixture Secretary, this was getting better by the minute. He wandered off towards the far end of the ground, desperately trying not to explode. One or two of the Brindon fielders could also see the funny side of things, and headed in a similar direction. They sat down in a small group. There were four or five of them altogether, and they just laughed until they cried. They witnessed and heard lots of screaming. Both on the pitch, where the umpires had by now got involved, in trying to restrain Des and their stumper. And also down at the scoreboard, where Bill was having a right go at Moaner and Nutter.

While watching proceedings from afar, one of the Brindon guys told Trainset that the wicket-keeper was a beer swilling hard case, and that his family were always in trouble with the law. This at least partly explained Blondie's character traits, but it still didn't stop the group thoroughly enjoying themselves for the next five or ten minutes.

The game eventually got under way again. But only after certain compromises were made between Bill and the Brindon Captain. It was agreed between the Skippers and Umpires that these 'rules' would apply, whether they were considered right or wrong.

Firstly Des had to be 'injured,' and walk off 'retired hurt.' He didn't like this one bit, of course. But at least it meant that he could protect Young Tim from further sexual advances.

And also protect his own batting average. Secondly their keeper had to apologise to all and sundry for his verbal outburst. Thirdly the score-box was to be locked up, and Young Tim and Blondie had to continue the scoring process from a more open position in the deckchairs. Fourthly the score was to be agreed as being 63 after thirteen overs. Fifthly Trainset was told to stop stirring things up, and to 'act like a proper twenty-seven-year-old, not like a pathetic weedy little twenty-seven-month-old.' And lastly the game was to be reduced to thirty-eight overs per side, to take account of the delays.

Barmfield eventually made 206 for five, off their 38 overs. Trainset knocked up 43, and Omar top scored with 63. So they had done OK.

The tea break was conducted in rather unusual circumstances. The atmosphere could have been cut with a knife. Blondie and Young Tim were closely chaperoned by their respective fathers. The full story of Trainset's stirring involvement had by now run around the players. Omar, Nutter and several of the Brindon guys wanted to treat him like a hero, but were embarrassed to break the silence. Others, such as Bill, Des and the Brindon Skipper, stared at him with complete disdain. And the opposition stumper honestly looked as though he wanted to kill him. 'Oh well,' the Plumber thought discretely. 'I can always join another club, I suppose. I've always got on quite well with the Danton Over Stale crowd.'

The Brindon innings was a bit of a fiasco. They only amassed forty-eight in total. The top scorer was the keeper, with a belligerent fifteen. Dave took six wickets, Omar the other four. Hypo got six catches.

Everyone began packing up to leave, and Bill was, as usual, 'squirting it on all over'. The fact that the game was now history had calmed things down slightly. Even Blondie's Dad was trying to be a bit more pleasant, possibly due to his top-scoring role. More to the point for Trainset, Des was much less agitated. The Fixture Secretary looked out of the Changing Room window, and he spotted Young Tim and

Blondie saying their farewells. They were clearly now getting on very well.

Trainset decided that the time was right for him to summon up the courage to speak to Des. He saw that his opening partner was on his own. So he took a deep breath and sidled up.

What the Number Two Batsman wanted to say was that, because Des wasn't as open-minded about things as the rest of them, he'd overreacted and got too wound up. But he knew that telling him all that lot would prove to be much too deep for Des to appreciate, so he just kept it to the more obvious statements.

'Look at Young Tim and Blondie, Des. They seem really happy. I know that I've been winding you all up, and I apologise for that. But I reckon that those two would have been friends by now anyway, whether I'd stirred things or not. They'd have been sitting together in that score-hut all afternoon, whether I'd said anything, or kept my mouth shut. You might not like the girl, Des. I can understand that; that's your prerogative. But you can't force Young Tim to not like someone just because you hate her, yourself, can you? I reckon that Blondie is like she is because of her stupid Dad, and because of this soul-destroying village. But at least she's got a bit of life in her, which must be difficult, living in this place. In any case, how do you know that Young Tim's not got ten girlfriends at school, all of them the same as Blondie?'

There was not a lot of feeling in Des's response. He spoke very clearly, and very precisely. There was no softness in his voice. It was all very matter of fact. 'At the end of the day, Trainset, you're sticking your nose into Tim's business, and also into mine. You may be correct in what you say, but it's got nothing to do with you. Has it? So I'm still really annoyed with you. In fact, it's a good job that we've been friends for years; otherwise I'd smack you one. And I still think that she's a cheap little tart, and that she's not good enough for my son. Let's leave it that, shall we?'

They left it at that.

Deputy Editor Ted Carruthers had by now left twenty messages on the answerphone of 'That Stupid Blasted Plumber'. And Steve Smith was beginning to feel a bit guilty that he'd not yet been in touch with his employer. He knew that he ought to let the fat idiot know where he'd got to. So he reluctantly phoned the Evening Gazette.

'Hello. How's it going, Steve?' asked Fatso.

'I'm up to Match Fifteen', answered the caller, hoping to get away with his little white lie.

'I know you, Steve. If you say that you've done fifteen, that means you've really only done about five. You'd better get a move on. See you in a week or so', said Lardo. 'Phone me when you're done.'

The phone slammed down. The conversation had ended somewhat abruptly. Ted Carruthers was clearly not overly happy with the timekeeping of his editorial protege.

The pressure was now on. The old scorebook told Steve that it was now time to bring Moaner into the limelight. But this one was going to be a bit more difficult. Particularly because the Plumber still kept in contact with Moaner. In fact the ex Barmfield Opening Batsman obtained some of his plumbing work through Moaner's recommendations. So Steve was a bit loath to go too far with his critique of Moaner. But he wanted his book to be good. As he recommenced The Definitive Works Of Plumber Smith, he muttered to himself. 'Oh well, if Moaner sues me, he sues me. Let's just get on with it...'

CHAPTER THIRTEEN
MATCH TWELVE

A WHITER SHADE OF PALE

John 'Moaner' Wickham was an inexplicable sort of guy. He was a natural at most sports, albeit that he was now getting a bit long in the tooth. He'd enjoyed a good life. He was still slim and athletic, despite his 47 years. His previously dark hair was now greying, and his face was showing signs of a few too many continental holidays, but he still looked very fit. He was a very successful businessman, having his own architectural practice. In fact he had everything going for him; huge house, attractive wife, great kids, etc. For Barmfield he usually batted at four, and, more often than not, scored runs. The problem with Moaner was that he just didn't seem to have the capacity to be nice to anyone. Like all male sports teams, Barmfield players enjoyed the regular rounds of mickey-taking banter, which only rarely upset any of them. But Moaner always seemed to be a bit nastier with it, somehow.

With a strong combination of experience and cricketing technique, he had been an obvious candidate to be the regular Captain, for years on end. He had more cricketing ability in his little finger than a hundred Bill's had in the whole of their bodies. But where Bill's man-management skills were excellent, Moaner's were buttock-clenchingly poor. In fact, Moaner's were non-existent.

The Club had once mistakenly given Moaner a taste of the captaincy, about four years ago, but he had cocked it up in a big way. After only 6 matches, he had upset all of them, several times over. And the team were heading for relegation. They had to call an emergency meeting at which he was 'asked to resign,' and Dave Jones was almost bullied into taking over.

Many of the others had thought that this episode would be the end of Moaner at their club, but amazingly he had just come back for more. Trainset was pretty sure that if he'd been booted out after just 6 games, he'd have left for pastures new. But such events were just water under the bridge to Moaner. And he still whinged and whined about everybody's performance, as much now as he used to do before being made Skipper, probably more so. To the rest of the team Moaner was a very strange guy.

Today Barmfield were playing at Tutburn. They were now comfortably fourth in the Division, and could head skywards if they won this one. Tutburn had a beautiful ground, with a castle and river as a backdrop. Visiting them was always one of the highlights of the Barmfield fixture list. And Persil wasn't attending today either, which made it even better.

Bill won the toss, and decided to field first. There was a reason for this decision, in that Des had phoned in to say he'd be a bit late, due to a family problem. Bill decided that he must have Des to open, so he'd chosen to insert the opposition. Trainset mused that, had he been late instead of Des, Bill would no doubt have received a rollicking from Des for not batting first. But the boot was on the other foot today, and so Des would now be happy with Bill's captaincy policy.

'It's all one way traffic with Des,' the Plumber carped, under his breath.

Nutter and Dave opened with the ball. Dave got a wicket with his third delivery, caught behind by Hypo. That spurred Barmfield on, and they soon had Tutburn down to 75 for 8. Mick had been introduced into the attack, and had already taken three for ten. He was getting lots of spin and bounce.

Because they had won the week before, Bill was wearing his wig, and therefore was less likely to catch anything. Other than the Black Plague. But his skippership was, as usual, excellent. He always seemed to have the right bowler on at the appropriate point in the proceedings, and the most appropriate fielders in the correct positions. Apart from himself, of course, as it was difficult for Bill to be in the correct position wherever he stood. So he stayed at second slip, on the basis that the ball normally went fairly fast if it went there, and anyone else fielding in that position could also miss it as well. Trainset could just about understand Bill's inverted logic.

The Tutburn Number Ten came in, and decided that valour was the better part of discretion. He was a big beefy bloke, and was clearly their quickie. He whacked at every ball he received, and with a combination of good hits and a few slices through Bill's hands and feet, began to take the game away from Barmfield. It was now 157 for 8.

Not for the first time this season, Bill was in a dilemma. He clearly needed to change things. What he needed was someone to bowl something a bit different. He'd tried most of the normal bowlers, and he couldn't risk bringing himself on for a second spell in the same season; he knew that doing that would be pushing it a few miles too far. Des had by now arrived on the pitch, so it was going to have to be one of Des, Moaner or Trainset. None of them had ever bowled in a proper match, so Bill was basing his thoughts on what he'd seen in the nets.

Bill looked thoughtfully at all three of them. Trainset could sense that it was a case of 'Who's the least pathetic of that appalling bunch of losers?' He recalled the last net session, when half of his own leggies landed ten yards behind the back net. Which was approximately fifteen yards behind the batsman. And Des and Moaner hadn't exactly shone that evening either. In fact they spent much of the session arguing about whether Des threw it or not. Of the whole Club, only Moaner thought that Des was a chucker. The fact no one else could care a toss, about whether he was a thrower or not, didn't stop Moaner going on and on about it. He was being pedantic, as usual. Moaner and Des hated each other.

Being something of a pessimist, Trainset thought through the likely results if he were to be given the ball. His bowling to their big hitter would be a repeat of Nash versus Sobers. All things considered, a whole lot worse, because he'd probably have to bowl about twenty-five deliveries to enable six of them to land on the track. And most of those six would be dropping vertically from thirty feet above the square. Nottinghamshire's Bomber Wells used to have a reputation of tossing them up a bit; the Barmfield Fixture Secretary tossed them up a lot.

Trainset started to panic. He started hobbling and rubbing his ankle, just to put further doubt in Bill's mind. But he needn't have worried. Bill had already made his decision. 'Come and have a go, Moaner.'

The Barmfield Number Two Batsman could relax. This was now an ideal scenario. If Moaner succeeded, then it would be great, at least from a team point of view. If he didn't, they could all sledge him mercilessly, and hopefully get their own back for some of the nasty things that he'd said to them over the years. So Trainset and the rest of the Barmfield fielders viewed proceedings with mixed feelings. Moaner practiced his off break 'run up'. He was ready to go.

By the third ball it was all over. Moaner had taken two for none. On the one hand Trainset was genuinely chuffed, on the other he felt a bit cheated. Bill and Moaner both walked off the field with something of a swagger. Moaner because he considered that he'd proved that he was not only their best bat, but also their best bowler; Bill because he'd taken a huge risk in putting the team prat on to bowl in the first place, and he'd been proved right.

Barmfield needed 158 to win. Not overly difficult, but not simple either.

The start of the batting reply must have appeared like an excerpt from the Best Of Fred Karno. Des pummelled his first ball straight into gulley's rather large stomach. Standing at the other end, Trainset didn't think the bloke genuinely saw it until it flopped out into his hands, which were still poised awaiting Des's initial stroke. The Number Two was then himself caught at mid-on, playing about five seconds too early. Not for the first time. And Omar swiped an awful shot across the line, and saw his stumps shattered by the big bloke who'd scored all their runs. Eleven for three. Whoops.

The Fixture Secretary could see it all coming. Moaner was going to win them the match, and they'd never hear the last of it. Trainset sat in a deckchair to watch events unfold.

Moaner and Vic set about repairing the damage. They got to 61 before Vic tried to run a quick second, tripped over his unfastened shoelace, and was run out by a good ten yards. Why he always batted in ill-fitting and broken kit, looking like some sort of bedraggled tramp, never ceased to amaze Trainset. The players had by now found out the reasons why he was always tired, and most of them had greatest of sympathy for the bloke. But it still didn't stop them being surprised to see him playing as though he was already enjoying the afterlife.

Tantrum was quickly in, and even more quickly out. It was a pity that he never seemed to give himself a chance to get a look at the bowling. He could be so good, but every week it was bash bang wallop from the first ball. He was bowled, again by the big Number Ten. 64 for 5.

Dave Jones came in and batted splendidly. He'd rattled up 25 in no time at all, until Number Ten got him caught, fencing at a short one. 95 for 6.

The normally reliable Hypo didn't last long either, falling lbw to the big chap. 102 for 7.

Bill entered the fray, to rapturous applause from his

thousands of adoring fans. Well Omar and Trainset, anyway. And the Fixture Secretary would have to admit that there might have been some slight sarcasm in their worship. Bill was bowled third ball, apparently off a very faint inside edge, by their medium pacer.

'Well at least I hit it,' Bill announced proudly, on his return. 'Which is more than can be said for you, Omar.' 102 for 8.

Moaner was still there. He'd not got lots of runs, but he was still there. And at last he found an able ally in Mick, who stuck it out, while Moaner gradually chipped away at the total. They crawled to 146 for 8. Mick then received a snorting yorker from Big Boy, and things were again looking rather black. It was now twelve to win, off three overs, and with last man Nutter on his way to the crease. But with 'That miserable git Moaner' still there, Trainset knew that they were still in with a shout.

The others found out later that, as Nutter walked up to take guard, Moaner had announced something along the lines of 'Don't worry, Nutter. Just get a single somehow, and then I'll finish it off. Before you get out as usual.' The opposition Captain brought up all his fielders to try to save one. But Nutter found a gap between the bowler and mid-off, which got Moaner down to the other end.

Moaner then did exactly what he said he'd do. He spanked three successive boundaries, and that was that.

Tutburn had their own bar, and Barmfield were in celebratory mood. Everyone was complimenting everyone else; well everyone except Moaner that is. Trainset could never understand why, but the better that Moaner personally performed, and the more beer that he drank, the less he seemed to think of the rest of them. Notwithstanding his impeccable one-man band performance, he was still having a right go at Bill and Des about Barmfield's lack of bowling abilities. In a very drunken voice. Nutter was out of earshot, and so it was he who was getting the greatest criticism from Moaner.

'I'm a much better bowler than he is, Phil. Er, Bill. In fact, if he's picked again next week, I'll eat my flaming fikscher carp, er card,' slurred Moaner.

Bill had something of a glint in his eye, as he replied. 'Moaner, you are living in the past. Either that, or being as pissed as a newt has affected your memory. Last year we had sixteen people to choose from. But you seem to have forgotten that we are really struggling for players this year. We haven't got the luxury of being able to change the team. As of now, it's always got to be the same eleven of us. So Nutter has already been picked for next week. Sorry, Moaner.'

From being fed up to the back teeth listening to Moaner whingeing on and on, Omar and Trainset were now beginning to take a great deal more interest in where this conversation was heading.

'Right, Bob,' said Moaner to his Captain, in a yet more slurred voice. 'I'm going to eat my fiksher carp then.'

What Moaner thought he was going to achieve by this expression of discontent, Trainset had no idea. And neither did he care. He rapidly dragged everyone around, to witness the event.

'I'd take the staples out first, if I were you, Moaner,' suggested Omar. Followed by 'I'll get you another pint, to wash it down,' from Mick. Trainset's own contribution was 'Shall I phone the ambulance now, or after you've swallowed it?'

Moaner ate the fixture card. It was downed along with another couple of pints. It took him quite a while to chew the rather thick document, especially the cardboard cover, but he did eventually finish the whole lot. The rest all cheered wildly as he went outside to regurgitate the offending paperwork.

'You might be better off getting a new fixture card now, Moaner, rather than using that one again,' shouted Des gleefully, through the still open door. Like Trainset, Des was happier than most to witness Moaner's demise.

Moaner was regularly sick during the evening, much to the amusement of Omar and Trainset. 'A Whiter Shade Of Pale' was sung enthusiastically and often, whilst the unfortunate Number Four puked away on the patio. The leader of the

Barmfield Procul Harum Fan Club was, as usual, Trainset. But the Number Two wasn't quite so happy later, when he drew the short straw, by being selected to 'Drive the idiot home.' Before he did so, and just to be safe, Trainset pre-covered his car seats with Moaner's cricket kit.

On arriving in Battenborough, the Fixture Secretary dragged Moaner out of his car, rang the front door bell, and left him there, unconscious, and covered in the results of his vomiting procedures.

The Barmfield players heard later that Moaner's wife wasn't very happy when she answered to the sound of the Frank Lloyd Wright Architectural Front Door Chimer at 11.30 that evening. But the Barmfield blokes were universally content. Not only had Moaner won them the match, but he'd also made himself look a complete cretin. And they'd all enjoyed that, immensely.

According to Bill, they were now third.

Steve The Perfect Plumber was pleased to get Moaner out of the way. Now it was the turn of Biased Bob. No doubt Bob would have died years ago, so there was less likelihood of negative reaction...

CHAPTER FOURTEEN
MATCH 13

WITH A LITTLE HELP FROM MY FRIENDS

Biased Bob was Barmfield through and through, which the others recognised as being the fundamental part of the problem. None of the side thought that his decision-making was intentionally biased towards them; it was more that he subconsciously still seemed to think that he was opening the batting for Barmfield. And also because he was just starting to get a bit past it.

Biased Bob had married Janet at a young age, but Dave didn't come along until Biased Bob was past the thirty mark. Apparently Biased Bob had later brought Dave to the matches more often than he'd brought Janet. He clearly considered cricket to be very much a man's sport, and he still seemed to enjoy the comradeship. His pensionable age didn't really come into it.

Biased Bob was smallish in stature. He had short greying hair, and a small moustache. His face was heavily lined; he'd spent much of his life outdoors in the sun. He wore glasses, but the lenses weren't overly thick. Not being aware of any optical imperfections, the Barmfield players considered that Biased Bob's on-field errors were more to do with his heart than with his eyes.

Trainset personally didn't know him too well, as Biased Bob tended to socialise more with the older guys such as Mick Fork. The umpire nearly always joined the team for a drink afterwards, but usually preferred to sit quietly in the corner. The Fixture Secretary thought that Biased Bob would have liked to reminisce about the olden days, if the others had ever given him the chance to do so. Perhaps they should have done. All Trainset had heard about Biased Bob was that the old codger's life seemed to centre around Barmfield, Janet, his dog and his allotment, very much in that order of priority.

If Biased Bob made what others considered to be a bad umpiring decision, it didn't appear to overly bother him. He'd brush off any verbal aggro, and carry on with the game as if nothing had happened. Trainset didn't think that he could have done that; he'd have worried all afternoon about just one mistake. Whether Biased Bob knew that most of the opposition teams considered him to be the most one-sided umpire in the League, Trainset hadn't a clue. But, if he did, he certainly never seemed to let it get to him. The Number Two Batsman was receiving vibes that Dave was now starting to be a bit embarrassed about things, particularly as he was personally becoming Barmfield's leading light on the playing side.

Barmfield were at home against Bardon Under Trent. Bardon were usually a very strong outfit. If Barmfield could beat them, it would be a massive win.

It was a hot day. Trainset was one of the last to turn up, having been stuck in traffic. Only Vic seemed to be missing, so most of the players were already changed and practicing on the outfield. As the Fixture Secretary walked past the group of opposition players and towards Stalag 9, he could see that Bill was in celebratory wig wearing mode, and that Tantrum seemed to be enjoying life. Nutter had a spring in his step, and even Moaner appeared to be sporting a very unusual slight grin, no doubt due to his runs the week before. Things were looking good.

The Plumber had almost reached the pavilion door, when a typical Saturday afternoon insult was hurled at his back.

'Nice of you to turn up, Trainset. Didn't think that you were going to bother today, you lazy honky. Have you been playing with your Hornby Double O?' It was that idiot Omar, having a go about the Plumber's timekeeping. 'Piss off back to the ruddy jungle,' Trainset countered, rather unkindly. Followed by 'And take that stupid prat of a wife with you. And feed her to the effing lions.'

Honky went in to get changed. Hoping that Persil wasn't in attendance, or at least that she hadn't heard his comments. In the changing room he saw Biased Bob sitting alone, reading an old scorebook. Trainset started first. 'Afternoon, Bob. How's things?'

'Hello Trainset' came a rather sad, distant reply.

Trainset began changing as he spoke. 'It's a hot one today, Bob. I hope they bat first. Have we tossed up yet?' He put on his whitish shirt and his greenish trousers. There was no further response from the umpire. Biased bob seemed to be miles away. So the Number Two Batsman just carried on doing his own thing. He left Biased Bob sitting there, as he jogged out to join the rest of the lads in the sun.

Barmfield did bat first. As Des purposefully strode out to the middle, leading his Number Two in tow like some sort of junior lapdog, Biased Bob took up his position at square leg. Bardon had a couple of good opening bowlers, so Des and Trainset had an important job to do. As did Biased Bob.

It was only the third ball of the innings when the first Biased Bobism took place. Des clearly edged one to the keeper, who took a good low catch. The Bardon close fielders all went up for the appeal, many of them so confidently that they were running to congratulate the bowler as they did so. To everyone on the field, other than to Biased Bob, it was a definite clean catch from a definite clean edge.

'Not Out,' said Biased Bob, confidently.

To make matters worse, Des didn't walk off. He'd given that up the previous season when he'd got the bad end of a few wrong ones from both Biased Bob and opposition umpires. So the Bardon blokes now saw two devils in their midst. The first one was 'That cheating blind idiot Biased Bob Jones,' the other one 'That cheating fat idiot Des Price.' Insults rained in on Biased Bob and Des.

After a minute or two of name-calling, order was partially restored, and the over completed. At this point Trainset thought that he'd quietly ask Biased Bob why he'd not sent Des on his merry way. The answer was at least logical, if wrong.

'Firstly I reckon he might have hit it into the ground, so it could have been a bump ball. And secondly I'm not sure that the keeper didn't catch it on the half volley. And remember, Trainset, we haven't got television replays at Barmfield.'

This document won't go through every error that Biased Bob made that day. Suffice to say that he was even worse than usual. And that's saying a lot. Decision after decision seemed to be wrong, and, more to the point, most of the cock-ups favoured Barmfield, rather than Bardon. So it was no surprise when Barmfield won the game, by over 50 runs. The star man was again Dave, with both bat and ball, but his superb performance only served to further highlight the problems created by his father.

At the end, the Bardon players were almost hysterical in their abuse of 'Bloody cheating Barmfield, and their bloody cheating umpire.' It was so bad that they not only refused to shake hands, but, much more significantly, they also refused to go to the pub. Their Skipper told Bill to expect a letter of complaint, a copy of which would be sent to the League. The Bardon umpire, who had not had a particularly good game himself, was the only one who had any sympathy for Biased Bob. He tried to calm the visiting players, by stating that 'We all make mistakes,' but he was shouted down as he did so. Dave noticeably kept well away from the fray.

As the Barmfield blokes got changed, not one of them was over-excited about winning. It was very much a hollow victory, given the circumstances. And Trainset also got the feeling that the afternoon's events were not yet over. They couldn't let this umpiring problem fester any longer. He was sure that something even more dramatic was about to take place. And so it proved.

Omar and Trainset reached The Noseblower first. They sat down over their first pint, and, as the rest of the Barmfield players drifted in, the two best mates went through their normal repertoire of black versus white abusive remarks. This week they concentrated their efforts on sexual aspects, such as relative penis sizes and the advantages of not wearing underpants in the jungle. Usually such a racialist tirade would bring out some interest and encouragement from such as Tantrum or Nutter, but no one was in much of a mood for it. So Omar and Trainset shut up. Last into the bar were Dave and Biased Bob. They bought their drinks, and shuffled quietly over to join the others.

After a minute or two of boring pleasantries, Dave came out with a not unanticipated announcement.

'My Dad's calling it a day. He'll finish off the season, but we'll need to find someone else for next year.'

Most of the players looked at Biased Bob. He was squirming about in his seat, and staring at the ground. Trainset suspected that he was trying to hold back the tears. His moustache was certainly quivering. It looked like a worm that had been dug out of the lawn. Dave went on.

'It's not just that he's had a couple of bad games this season. It's a bit worse than that. His eyesight's going. The doctors think that it might be the onset of some form of full blindness. He's got to have further tests yet, but it doesn't look good. We didn't want to say anything until the end of the season, because the team is doing so well. But today's events have made us think again.'

The players were all taken aback. Biased Bob had given

some stupid decisions in the last two or three years, and this year he had been very, very poor. But there hadn't been any clue that he was ill. The sympathies began to flow.

'I'm sorry to hear all that, Bob,' said Vic. 'If you ever need any counselling from either me or my Boss, just let me know.' The others sort of assumed that the 'Boss' in question was the one in the sky, as opposed to the Area Bishop, or Vic's Missus. But none of them were too sure what Vic meant, as was often the case.

Bill joined in. 'I'm shocked, Bob. If it helps, I've got several books on optical illnesses. I'll lend them to you, if you want.' He then added, somewhat unkindly, 'Assuming that you can still read, of course.'

And so it went on. They all sympathetically expressed their feelings, and most of them offered something else more practical as well. For instance, Moaner said that he'd draw up plans for a downstairs loo, for free. Following on from this idea, Trainset suggested that he'd install any necessary bathroom equipment, again at no cost. Hypo told Biased Bob that, despite having his own serious eye condition, along with numerous other long-term problems, that he'd also help electrically. As long as regular free food was to be provided, of course.

But Nutter seemed to have somehow missed the point, when he finished off the first round of responses with his personal offer of assistance. 'If you ever need any carrots, Bob, I can get you them buckshee, from my mate at the sewage works. He grows them behind the site office, at the end of the sewer that comes from the Wollatown estate. Carrots are good for eyesight, Bob. Shall I just bring a ton to start with? You might just have to rinse them a bit first.' Casting aside his own problems, Biased Bob raised a slight smile at that one, sending his moustache into further worm-like balletics. Whilst politely refusing Nutter's kind offer.

Dave described the technicalities of the optical diagnosis. The rest of them all nodded and emitted intelligent sounding responses, like 'OK,' or 'Oh dear,' at what they considered to be an appropriate point. Trainset guessed that none of them really had any idea what Dave was talking about; the Fixture Secretary certainly didn't. He also had the feeling that Dave realised that he was talking to a bunch of boneheaded imbeciles, but that he still wanted to get things off his chest, anyway. So the star all-rounder just carried on. Eventually he finished by repeating that Barmfield would now need another umpire for the following season.

The atmosphere was getting gloomier. Biased Bob tried to lift their spirits. He feigned optimism, when he spoke. 'Not to worry. I'll get by with a little help from my friends.' Such a statement didn't really seem to represent what he must have been feeling, but at least Biased Bob was trying to appear positive. And his words did yet again re-emphasise how much Barmfield Cricket Club meant to him.

While Biased Bob nipped to the lavatory, everything went very, very quiet. They supped at their pints in an almost embarrassing silence. It was all rather dramatic. Before today, they'd had an elderly guy in their midst, one who the rest of them had loved to laugh at, and to criticise. He'd unwittingly played the Dad's Army Corporal Jones character. Now they all forlornly wished that they hadn't sniggered behind his back, but rather that they'd taken a more genuine interest in his stories about the Barmfield teams of 30 years previous.

On Biased Bob's return, Hypo broke the silence. It was a stroke of genius on his part.

'What happened about that quiz the other week, Bob? Did Janet get anywhere with her applications to the TV companies?'

Biased Bob's reply was instantaneous, and supportively enthusiastic. 'Yes, Hypo. Thanks for asking. Janet didn't want to do it, so I made contact myself, with all the main TV channels. I haven't told her yet, but I heard yesterday that she's got a screen test for Mastermind.' Biased Bob turned towards his son. 'Thinking about it, I haven't had chance to tell you, either, Dave. I'm well chuffed. It gives us an interest, which should help us through all this.'

They all relaxed a bit. 'Well done Hypo. Nice one,'

thought Trainset.

Normal conversation restarted. Trainset suggested that, as Fixture Secretary, he should write to Bardon, explaining things. But the consensus was that it might be better if someone also contacted them by telephone first, before Bardon's own letter went off to the League Committee. Bill agreed to take on that particular task, stating that he'd phone their Skipper the following day. Knowing how angry their Captain was, Trainset was pleased that his own contribution was only to be a written one.

As he left The Noseblower, Trainset couldn't help but notice that Tantrum, Mick and Des were still there, firing question after question at Biased Bob, about Barmfield characters of the 1950's. Human beings are a bit predictable really, aren't they?

It was Allesbush next week, and they all hoped that cricket would take over again.

The next evening, Steve was back on the computer. 'Right. It's back to the players now. This match was about Mr Dexter Ruddy Price. And I feature quite strongly as well. This should be the best one of the lot.'

He typed avidly...

CHAPTER FIFTEEN
MATCH 14

THE BEST THING THAT EVER
HAPPENED TO ME

Dexter Price was, in Trainset's opinion, a really good bloke. Not everyone agreed, as Mr Price had been known to fall out with one or two. Known simply as 'Des,' his weakness, and probably also his strength, was that he was just too honest. He always called a spade a spade, and some of the guys didn't like that. If someone played well, Des would praise him. If another didn't, Des was not slow to criticise. But his criticism wasn't as nasty as the abusive brickbats thrown by Moaner. It was all much more 'fatherly' in its style. In fact the Fixture Secretary was of the view that Des saw the rest of the team as his own family of boys. Trainset, and one or two of the others, rather enjoyed the comradeship of the firm, but very fair, Des Price.

Des was a similar age to Bill. He was also, like Bill, some sort of salesman. But whereas Bill drove around in a Jag, and was, on the face of it anyway, rolling in cash, Des seemed to have to work hard for his middle of the range Ford. Trainset considered Bill to be a very bright chap, who would always find an easy way to earn a good crust. In contrast, he thought of Des as very much an ordinary bloke, who'd done OK, and was very proud of what he'd achieved in life. But he was never going to be a millionaire, or, for that matter, an Einstein.

To Trainset, Des seemed rather Yorkshireman-like in attitude, but whether he originated from the White Rose County, no one knew. He was solid in build, and solid in character. He had thinning fair hair, and a rather dumpy appearance, which belied the strength in his forearms.

Des took his cricket seriously. Very seriously. He was always immaculate in his cricketing attire, not quite as immaculate as the Persil-inspired Omar, but immaculate enough. And like Bill, he had his own bat, the difference between the two men being that Des did have some idea of how to use his. Des was Vice-Captain to Bill, and they got on reasonably well.

Des was also good at boring everyone to tears, with deep meaningful insights into the details of the Laws of Cricket. Trainset thought that his opening partner might eventually write his own less than scintillating book on the subject. But if he did, and if it sold more than two copies, then Trainset would be astonished. Such a tome would have about as much reader interest as a plastic goldfish.

Des often played in midweek for various social or business teams. So, in effect, he'd played cricket twice a week every summer for thirty odd years. But, up until this day, Des had never scored a century. Trainset could see that Des's cricket was so important to him that, should the Number One ever score a hundred, he would surely die a happy man.

This particular Saturday the Barmfieldians were at Allesbush. It was a lovely day, and the pitch looked hard and fast. Trainset heard Des tell Bill 'I reckon we could get a few runs here.' How right he was.

Bill won the toss, and chose to bat first. Unusually, there was no criticism of this decision, not even from Moaner. Des and Trainset opened the innings, and runs started to flow. Because it was so hot, there was a drinks break after twenty overs, at which point the score had already reached ninety-eight for no wicket. Tantrum and Vic brought out the refreshing cold orange juice, and they had quiet words with both batsmen, instructing them to 'Keep up the good work', and 'Don't throw it away now.'

The two openers didn't 'throw it away'. The Number Two hammered away on the leg side, Des did the same on the off. The Plumber was well in front of his partner at one point, having scored about eighty to Des's fifty or so. But then Des had a particularly purple patch, and he rattled up his second fifty in rapid time, thereby beating Trainset to a century.

Des's face at that moment was an absolute picture. Trainset shook his hand, so did several of the fielders. The deckchairs were full of applause and shouts of encouragement. Tantrum started wolf-whistling, and shouting 'Come on you Barmfields.' A bit embarrassing, but it was Tantrum, after all. Of everyone watching from the pavilion, it was noticeable that only Moaner was not showing any great enthusiasm for Des's efforts.

Des looked so proud of himself that Trainset could have cried. In fact, he almost did. It seemed to be that, at that point on that day, Des just took stock of his life. Walking around the stumps, waving his bat at all and sundry, he was in a regal mood. In his mind he was playing at Lords, against Australian or West Indian superstars. The Barmfield Number One Batsman seemed to be running through the personal ramifications of his effort. Trainset read it as something along the lines of 'Well done Des. You've got a good wife, a good job, and good kids. And now you've achieved the only big goal left that you ever had. I'm proud of you, Des.'

The Fixture Secretary followed all this excitement up with his own ton, which was perhaps a bit of an anti-climax after the events of ten minutes before. At the end of the innings,

Young Tim was pleased to announce that Barmfield had totalled 242 for none, Des scoring 121, his partner only 'a relatively mediocre 116'. So 'Dad had done far better than that gob-shite Trainset'. There weren't many extras conceded by Allesbush, their keeper having done extraordinarily well on such a hot day.

Des and Trainset swaggered off to a standing ovation from all and sundry, Moaner excepted. Des's grin had to be seen to be believed. It was from ear to ear. Or should one say from ear protector to ear protector.

On reaching the changing room, it was obvious that Des and the Number Two were both very hot. In fact they were both sweating profusely. Des decided that a quick shower was in order, whilst his partner preferred to lap up the praise. Tea was therefore taken without Des. Trainset was still on such a high that eating was difficult. Whilst pouring, at breakneck speed, several cups of hot tea down a desperately dry throat, compliments poured in upon him. Omar told the Plumber that it was the best innings that he'd seen from a half-witted honky idiot, Bill asked him why he'd not batted like that in any of his previous ten thousand innings, and Nutter suggested that the two openers could be in line to win the County Village League Annual Batting Prize. Well, he actually said 'County League Village Cup', but they all knew what Mr Brain of Britain (and Ireland) really meant. The tea ladies generously declined to mention any embarrassing bodily smells emanating from the Plumber, and instead told him how pleased they were for him.

However, the Fixture Secretary considered the comment from Hypo to be his favourite, and, in lots of ways, the most poignant. The wicket-keeper looked the Plumber in the eye, and only said a few words. But those few words meant an awful lot. 'I used to be a much better cricketer than you, Trainset. Now, I'm not so sure. Well done, mate.' That was massive flattery from his old school pal, a hugely significant point in the Plumber's cricketing life.

But it wasn't really Trainset's day. It was that of his partner in crime. A refreshed Des returned to the Tearoom just in time to catch the last piece of cake, and he was immediately besieged by well-wishers. In particular, he was thoroughly congratulated by Vic and Hypo, who both treated the Number One as some sort of king. However, Des could have done without the playful attentions of Nutter. As the Salesman tried to swallow the sultana and nut slice, the fast bowler, rather ill advisedly, patted him on the back. It was all in a friendly spirit, of course, but that wasn't the point. It took three or four of the others to prevent the hero of the moment from choking to death.

'You stupid prat, Nutter,' said Bill, with no little feeling.

Trainset, by now keeping well out of Nutter's way, managed to hastily down a couple more drinks before it was time for all of them to follow their Skipper back out on to the pitch. They formed a little huddle near the wicket.

'Right,' said Bill, as usual. 'We've done the first bit, now let's do the second.' Vice-Skipper Des tried to back up the comments, with his own little speech. But his throat would only allow him to return to choking mode.

'You stupid prat, Nutter,' aped Tantrum, to the beleaguered redheaded Irishman.

It was hard work 'Doing the second.' The Allesbush batsmen also fared well on the benign pitch. Nutter tried his heart out, bowling 12 overs of sheer pace on what was now a very hot late afternoon. The fast bowler would never admit it of course, but Trainset was strongly of the opinion that Nutter especially wanted to win this match, not for Barmfield in general, or for himself in particular. But for Des. Either because the fast bowler was delighted for the opening bat's achievement, or out of guilt because he thought that he'd nearly killed him. It was a stupendous effort from the red haired Irishman. Although Omar picked up a rare wicket, Barmfield only got three batsmen out, and at one stage it looked as though Allesbush might spoil the day by winning. In the end, however, Barmfield got their reward, succeeding by nineteen runs. None of the Allesbush blokes had scored a century, so the after-match talk was still about Des and Trainset.

The openers lapped up the praise. Photos were taken in front of the scoreboard, and Dave started to draft out an article for the local paper. Moaner commented that the efforts of their opening batsmen 'weren't too bad, although I think that they ought to have scored a lot more against tiring bowlers towards the end.' The Fixture Secretary was not sure whether this was the first compliment that he'd ever received from Moaner, or whether it was just yet another slight dig in the ribs. But he'd gone past bothering about 'Old Pratface's' opinions.

Trainset was not wishing to sound saint-like when he stated to all and sundry that he was honestly was much happier for Des than he was for himself. This was Des's day, and Trainset was just so pleased that he was the one who'd helped him do it.

The Plumber had a lump in his throat when he overheard Des talking to Bill. 'Today was the best thing that ever happened to me, Bill.'

They all had several drinks in the Allesbush Arms. Des then phoned his wife, and she arranged to turn up at The Noseblower for their celebratory return. Des was in generous mood. So much so, that he even took an alcoholic beverage out to Young Tim, who was sitting in his Dad's car, listening to the radio. It was only a half a pint of shandy, but Trainset saw this as a key step by Des, particularly as such a move was, of course, illegal. In Trainset's eyes, it meant that Des was now starting to think of his offspring as being a junior grown up, as opposed to being a grown up junior. The day's events had clearly affected Des in more ways than one; it was as though some sort of physical and mental restraint had been removed.

What a night they had. It was considered by all concerned to be one of the best ever.

At the end of such a momentous day in the history of Barmfield Cricket Club, they were still third. But second spot was now becoming closer. Things were starting to get very, very exciting in Division Two South.

The facts and figures in the scorebook for the penultimate game of the season gave the Plumber an opportunity to have a go at Parvar Singh. During that summer, Parvar had been the bane of Steve's life, and that of many of the others, as well...

CHAPTER SIXTEEN
MATCH 15

HEY GIRL, DON'T BOTHER ME

Parvar Singh was Omar's wife. They had got married over the previous winter. The players nicknamed her 'Persil,' because of her obsession with cleanliness.

Persil was tall, slim and elegant. She had a model-like appearance, with big brown eyes, long black hair and perfect teeth. She was therefore pleasantly attractive to look at. But, not only in the view of Trainset, she was utterly unattractive in every other respect. Omar and Trainset had been best mates for years. But when Persil entered the scene, Omar seemed to change character overnight. Once a free-speaking, free-drinking, laugh-a-minute sort of a guy, he'd now become much more serious and circumspect, particularly when Persil was in sight, or in earshot.

Persil was a few years older than Omar, and she was a very domineering sort of a person. Again, the Fixture

Secretary wasn't the only one who thought so. Quite what Omar saw in her, Trainset would never be able to fathom. Putting the boot on the other foot, he couldn't understand what she saw in Omar, either, because her ambitions for herself weren't reflected by Omar's position in life, or in his true personality. Persil had been born to wealthy parents, and already had her own business, a high quality fashion shop in the nearby city. Her plans were to own a lot more of them, and eventually to have outlets in every town in the country. Omar, on the other hand, was from a poor immigrant family, and he had no obvious ambitions at all. At least he hadn't before he met Persil.

So, apart from being similar in terms of geographical background, and skin colour, Omar and Persil were otherwise poles apart.

Persil had several other traits that several of the team weren't overly keen about.

Firstly she was pedantic in what she wanted for herself, and for Omar, and was one of those people that always had to be proved right. She'd argue the toss forever if one of the others had the temerity to question one of her loudly voiced opinions. Such a person was always going be difficult to converse with, and several of the Barmfield lads secretly thought that under her thick outer skin was a much, much, thicker brain. They considered that the reason for her forthrightness was the fact that she wasn't bright enough to see or understand the viewpoints of others.

Secondly she was fastidiously clean. Omar's cricket kit had now become a sight to behold. So much so that he now appeared frightened to try to stop the ball in the field, in case he obtained a miniscule grass mark by doing so. And there was no way that he was ever going to wipe a disgustingly filthy red cricket ball on his trousers whilst he was bowling; that was mid-off's or mid-on's job from now on.

Thirdly, she was one of the few people that Trainset knew who owned a mobile phone. Vic had one, but never got it out of its leather wallet. But Persil was always using hers. Usually she was phoning out, talking at full volume to some unfortunate recipient or other. But occasionally her business contacts would phone her. So a Barmfield game would often have the feel of a busy office, rather than that of a cricket match. Persil was a very selfish person.

Finally Persil was also a complete pain in the backside in her supposed tea lady role. As previously mentioned, Sexy Sam was more than capable of doing this job on her own. And she also had Janet to help her. So she certainly didn't need an expert on all things culinary standing alongside her in the Tearoom, criticising her every move. It wasn't as though Persil made up for her comments by being particularly good, or useful. In fact Trainset had hardly ever seen her do any actual work. This was probably because she thought that she might possibly get slightly messed up by doing something degradingly menial, like buttering a slice of bread. Persil clearly drove the normally mild-mannered Sexy Sam absolutely mad, along with most of the rest of the Barmfield crowd.

Hopefully you've now got the picture of the team's opinion of Persil. In summary, they were unfortunately just stuck with the horrible woman, and most of them wished that they weren't.

Today Barmfield were at home against Friarbridge. This was to be the penultimate game of the season, so a win would put them well on course for the League Title. They were therefore taking this match very seriously. So seriously that most of them, for the first time this season, had taken part in proper net practice on both Tuesday and Thursday evening. They'd also given Mick's bowling machine another whirl. Well, they did so for about half an hour, at which point the mechanism developed some sort of technical hiccup and started to bowl 100mph beamers at Bill's wig. However, despite such enthusiasm by most of the team, there had been no sign of Omar at nets, no doubt due to the fact that Persil needed him to cook the evening meal every night. It was one thing being under the thumb, and totally another being under Persil's thumb.

There was a delay to the start of today's game. Heavy

overnight rain had continued into the morning. Mick, Bill, their Skipper and the umpires decided to 'give it half an hour to dry out a bit' before play commenced. The match was therefore reduced to 35 overs each.

Persil immediately took advantage of the delay. She collared two of the opposition female supporters, and started pestering them about how she could do them a good deal on high-end fashion. Trainset couldn't help but hear it, her voice being a cross between a well-known local Indian female politician, and a foghorn.

'I sell all the top brands. Only designer stuff of course, none of your high street rubbish. I've got friends in high places, you know. The top companies think I'm going to make it big. If you call around to my shop, I'll sort you out some decent stuff for your next cruise. At 20% discount. Just for you two, of course.'

Trainset winced, and he was pretty sure that Omar and Persil's female audience were doing something similar. But minor setbacks like that wouldn't deter Persil.

'Here's my card. Phone me soon. My company is called 'Beauty For The Discerning.' Tell you what, I'll walk around the ground with you and tell you more about it all. We can have a proper chat, away from this cricketing riff-raff.'

One of the two ladies tried desperately to avoid the pending nightmare. 'Oh. Thank you. But, er, I'm not in a hurry to buy, though. Er, I'd like to leave it for a while ......'

Persil cut her off. 'Don't be silly. Walk round the ground with me, and we'll have a little natter. I'm sure we can fix you up with something a damn sight better than the rubbish that you're wearing now. Come along, ladies. Walkies.'

And, with her rather unenthusiastic audience in tow, off she went.

Bill lost the toss, and Barmfield went out to field. Unusually, all eleven of them walked out together, because the half hour delay had meant that Vic was not now late. After the rain, it had turned into another nice day, and a larger than usual crowd had gathered. The deluge had left the outfield rather slippery, with a particularly muddy area down at long leg. Mick had previously covered the pitch itself, and the last few yards of the bowlers' run-ups, so the main areas were fine.

Nutter was to open from the Pavilion end. Barmfield took their fielding positions. Omar was to bowl the second over from the sightscreen end, so Bill sent him down to long leg. In other words, he was to field on the muddiest part of the outfield. Not the greatest idea, bearing in mind that Persil was around, but ours not to reason why.

Even worse was to come for Omar. When he arrived down at the long leg boundary, Persil was by now standing about five yards away from him, talking to the two Friarbridge ladies. Or should one say talking at the two Friarbridge ladies. Persil was immaculately dressed, as usual, wearing what was clearly a very expensive fawn coloured skirted suit, complete with equally posh brown leather boots. The other two were in old jeans and ordinary tops. No doubt Persil was still telling them how good her fashion shop was, and how they ought to call in for a free fitting, etc., etc., etc. She never was one to miss such an opportunity; so helping Sexy Sam and Janet with the teas could wait forever, as far as she was concerned.

It took just one ball for the fireworks to start. Nutter bowled a shortish delivery on leg stump, and the Friarbridge Number One flicked it off his hip down towards Omar.

It was a regulation single. Or it should have been. All Omar had to do was to wait for the ball to arrive, pick it up, and lob it back to Hypo. Which is exactly what he would have done prior to meeting Persil. But he panicked, no doubt because she was standing immediately behind him. He ran at the ball, and slipped, sliding about five yards on his backside, in the thick mud. The ball rolled gently past him, coming to a stop a few yards away, just inside the boundary rope, and only a few feet from Persil. Omar picked himself up, turned towards the ball, tried to accelerate, and slid again. For his second interpretation of a dying swan act, he was on his front, rather than his back. He flew straight into his beloved missus, and completely flattened her.

By the time the ball was eventually returned to Hypo, the batsmen had run six, Omar was covered from head to foot in brown slimy mud, Persil was lying on her back screaming her head off, Bill was having an apoplexy, and the rest of the Barmfield side were having an absolute field day. Particularly as Persil had by now realised that she had been exposing her £100 silk 'knickers and stockings' combo to the rest of the world.

Omar needed to get cleaned up. He trudged forlornly towards the pavilion. Unfortunately, he had to pass many of his team-mates on the way. So he couldn't easily avoid receiving several rather unkind comments.

A particularly good one came from Vic, who must have been a bit more awake than usual. He spoke, rather drolly. 'Your performance reminded him of a programme I saw on the TV the other night, Omar. It was about mating rituals of rhino buffalos. The male firstly rolls in the mud to excite the female, who then lies on her back, legs akimbo. The male then slides along the mud at the female. Very similar to your recent performance. Does your religion practice rhino buffalo-based sex techniques, Omar?'

Tantrum produced another corker. 'Perhaps your Missus makes more knicker sales if she models them herself, in front of fifty people on a public park, Omar? Presumably she was deliberately strength-testing the crotch for her audience?'

But Trainset thought the best remark came from Moaner. It was slightly racial in tone, but it was still very funny. 'I can't tell where you finish and your clothes start, Omar. Are you standing on your head?'

Omar continued his bedraggled and embarrassing walk towards Stalag 9, now having to pass the quivering deckchairs of Barmfield's opponents, who were desperately trying not to be seen openly laughing. Some of them were clearly failing in this respect.

Meanwhile, hobbling disconsolately around the far side of the ground, was Persil. She was limping, and being helped along by her two 'potential customers.' She was herself also completely bedraggled, her £500 suit now more resembling a fifty pence sackbag. And her £250 boots were clearly also of little use, as she was carrying one of them by its broken heel. She was making a lot of noise. Trainset couldn't tell from that distance whether it was crying, laughing, or just hysterical attention-grabbing screaming, but he'd have put money on it being the latter.

Being good at maths, he quickly calculated that, what with probable additional damage to such as her blouse and her necklace, Persil was about £1,250 worse off than she had been a few minutes earlier. But the damage to her self-righteous ego was, to all appearances, well into the millions. Trainset loved it. It was great. 'More, more, more,' he whispered excitedly.

Omar had an extremely rapid shower, and also quickly found some whites from the 'spare kit' box, and it was only five minutes or so before he was back out again. His equipment was obviously two or three sizes too small, so he looked a bit like an overgrown version of Dopey, out of The Seven Dwarves. But his rapid reappearance meant that he could continue to avoid Persil for another hour or two. In the current climate, looking like The Sugar Plum Fairy would have been a far more preferable option to Omar; the alternative was too awful to contemplate.

Persil neared the pavilion. She could now clearly be seen, and heard for that matter, going ballistic about all things cricket, but particularly about all things cricket, male and Kenyan. Limping around the deckchairs, she hurled abuse at all and sundry, threatening to 'sue this rotten mentally retarded Club,' and to 'get my marriage annulled.' All this seemed somewhat unfair on the Friarbridge visitors, as they had played no part whatsoever in her demise. But they were cricketers, so that was good enough for Persil.

At one point, Trainset heard Omar ask Bill if he could stay at the muddy end for the rest of the innings, so that he would remain at least 100 yards away from his demented wife. He also asked not to bowl. Bill had suffered enough from Omar already, so he willingly agreed to both requests.

Barmfield bowled and fielded very badly.   The Persil

incident had distracted them all, and Friarbridge had taken full advantage. Their visitors totalled 197 for 7 off their 35 overs, which was an excellent score, particularly on such a slow pitch.

At the tea break, Barmfield were very confident of what was to come. Unfortunately this was because they were very confident that they were going to lose. They headed dejectedly towards the refreshments. Bill was livid with them; several players received more than a bit of tongue-lashing as they trooped off towards Stalag 9. But the Fixture Secretary was not overly worried about Bill's comments towards him. He was much more interested in looking forward to witnessing round two of the Omar/Persil heavyweight title fight.

His hopes were, however, already dashed. Persil had left. Apparently she'd asked one of the two Friarbridge ladies to take her to A&E, and then on to her father's house. Before leaving, she'd left a message with Sexy Sam that 'Omar wasn't to expect her home that evening, or any other evening, for that matter.' And that she'd be 'asking her father to take legal action against Barmfield Cricket Club, on her behalf.'

The players all knew that Persil wouldn't stand any chance whatsoever in winning any sort of legal case against the club. But they also knew that her threat to leave Omar was another matter entirely.

Trainset reflected on recent events. 'It's amazing what effect exposing your knickers to all and sundry can have on a person. What on earth would have she have acted like, if she'd not been wearing any?' He decided not to go any further down that rather particular route, as he wanted to enjoy his tea.

Barmfield had, in front of a big crowd, up to now performed very badly. So, before Des and Trainset went out to bat, Bill gave them all a bit of a lecture. 'We've had a few problems this afternoon, chaps. Omar giving away five extra runs off that first ball didn't help matters. In fact it set the scene for a very poor performance in the field. If we want to win this

Division, we need to tighten things up a bit. In fact, we need to tighten things up a lot.' He then homed in specifically on his Number Two Batsman.

'You did well last week, Trainset. But that was last week. The pitch is a lot slower today, so I don't want to see any of those stupid skied drives of yours, for a start. Wait for the ball to arrive, before you swing at it. You aren't here just to give catching practice to the opposition, you know. We are trying to win a cricket League, not the world slapstick comedy championships.'

Next it was Des's turn. 'Des, well done for last week. Now forget it. Listen to me, for a change. We've got 35 overs to win this. Not 5 overs. None of that belligerent stuff to every ball outside off stump, please. Give it a good look first, for Christ's sake. Do you understand what I'm saying, Des? Are you actually listening, Des?'

And so it went on. Within five minutes, everyone had his particular batting style thoroughly dissected by Bill. The Barmfield Skipper was clearly on the ball in his abilities to pick out the faults of his team. It was a pity that he couldn't apply such expert critique to his own bat-handling abilities. Whether such a critical approach towards the rest of them would bear fruit a few minutes later was open to debate. It all seemed a bit harsh from their Captain, considering their superb performance of the previous week. But their fielding display this afternoon had rattled Bill in a big way, and now he was telling each of his players what he thought of them, in no uncertain terms.

Normally Bill's man-management skills were very good. But today's approach seemed, to Trainset anyway, to be a big risk. The Captain had really got to him, and the Plumber went out to bat with his brain full of conflicting thoughts about his batting technique. He was almost shaking with a complete lack of confidence, just waiting to make a mistake and face the wrath of their Skipper. Should he move his feet, and play his usual game? Or should he just stand there like a transfixed rabbit in car headlights? Bill's comments had put the wind up him. He was a quivering wreck, and he guessed that some of the others batters felt the same.

Trainset's fears proved well founded. It was 17 for 5 when Dave walked out to join Tantrum.

Not only was it pandemonium on the pitch, but it was pandemonium in the deckchairs as well. Bill was slagging everyone off, one by one. And they were doing the same back to him. It was a right dingdong affair. Sexy Sam slammed the Tearoom door shut, as an expression of her personal annoyance at the noise outside.

Trainset sat down on his own, in a bit of a sulk. In his view Bill had just got too wound up about it all. Sure, they wanted to win the title, but most of them wanted to enjoy themselves as well. The nearer they'd got to the winning post, the nastier it had all become. What they needed was to win the damned thing ASAP, and then they could all relax a bit.

He was suddenly woken from his meanderings.

'Great shot, Tantrum. Watch out Trainset.' The Number Two jumped out of the way just as the ball crashed into the wall behind him, narrowly missing the main Tearoom window. That was some hit from their Number Six.

The Fixture Secretary looked at the scoreboard. Amazingly they were now 66 for 5. It only seemed a few minutes ago when he was fifth out, bowled all over the place by their big opening bowler, with the score on 17. Things were starting to get back on track. 'Come on Tantrum,' he shouted. 'Let's have another.'

It got better and better. Dave had regular words with their sixteen-year-old prodigy, to calm him down. And Tantrum carried on hitting the ball to all parts of the ground. Trainset fetched Sexy Sam and Janet out to watch, so that they wouldn't miss witnessing the Barmfield innings of the season.

Barmfield won by four wickets, with six overs to spare. Tantrum was out just before the end, caught at deep square leg, for a truly magnificent 104. He had hit seven sixes, and eleven fours. He got a standing ovation from all and sundry. Dave only scored 57 not out, but it was his man management of Tantrum that was the key to the victory. Along with his complete mental dismissal of Bill's earlier criticisms of his batting inabilities. Dave had been superb, yet again. He was a very tough cookie, was Dave.

Omar had suffered an abominably bad day. His kit had been ruined, Bill had given him a right rollicking, he'd been the laughing stock of everyone at the ground, his missus had made a complete prat of herself, he'd had to wear an undersized straightjacket for most of the match, and he'd also got a first ball duck. Just to round things off nicely, he was also heading for a divorce.

But was he bothered? No, he was as happy as Larry. When he got to the pub he took it all in his stride, and he had a great laugh, and several beers. When Omar asked Trainset, for the umpteenth time 'Fancy another one, mate, you honky idiot?' his eyes were wide and bright again, and his brow was unfurrowed. This was the old Omar, in fact the real Omar, as far as the Plumber was concerned. The two of them were drunk enough to stand up and sing a beer-fuelled duet, a rousing chorus of 'Hey Girl Don't Bother Me.'

Trainset just hoped that pea-brained Persil would stick to what she'd said, and leave the poor bloke alone.

Barmfield looked like being Champions now.

The Plumber sat down at his desk. Perhaps crappy old garage bench would have been a truer description of his working facilities. Anyway, there was now a major decision to be made. Should he just get on with writing about Match 16? Or should he bring in a review of the Summer Fete. The problem with the latter option was that it would make him look a complete nerd. Going against his better judgement, he chose to describe the Fete…

CHAPTER SEVENTEEN
THE SUMMER FETE

KEEP ON RUNNING

It was by now the beginning of September. There was always a Saturday missing in Barmfield's League fixtures, to take account of the annual Barmfield Village Summer Fete. So the vital final match, against Battenborough, would have to wait for another week.

Each year, the Barmfield Village Summer Fete grew a little more grand. In the last twenty years, the cricket club had become more and more involved, and by now they had got themselves into a situation where they couldn't easily back out of their involvement in it. Particularly as, for the last decade or so, many of the happenings had taken place at the cricket ground. So the club fully participated in the day's events, though many of the team would rather not have done.

This year, the activities were to be spread over two venues. The church, along with the associated church hall, was to host the serious stuff, such as the flower arranging and art competitions. Whereas the cricket club was to be responsible for the more downmarket attractions, food stalls, fair rides, and so on.

The club always made a few quid out of the day, but not enough to justify the time and effort involved. One of the problems was that Mick was always whittling on about damage to the ground in general, and to the pitch in particular. So there was always a strong pre-fete element of protecting everything in sight. The square itself was completely boarded over, using costly hired timber and metalwork supports. To Trainset this massive ground protection effort reminded him somewhat of Des preparing to open the batting, although he could see rather more point to the former of the two exercises. Like the rest of the team, the Plumber wasn't very happy about the possibility of the local yobbos causing mayhem to what was very much his, and his team-mates', private Saturday afternoon entertainment venue. But, having said that, many of the Barmfield lads had been born in the village, and so had split loyalties regarding the annual event.

One relatively important point about this year's fete was that no more League games were to be played at Barmfield this season. This at least gave an eight-month recuperation period for any damage caused. Such a fact had not gone unnoticed by Mick, who was therefore slightly more relaxed about things than he had been in previous years.

The other positive side issue about the fete this year was that the cricket club appeared to be heading towards a successful conclusion to their season, which meant that there was likely to be a greater interest from the local public. More raffle tickets would doubtless be sold, and it could even be that one or two of the less imbecilic of the local tearaways might show some slight interest, by joining their mate Tantrum and attending the forthcoming winter indoor nets.

Every year, one of the more interesting aspects of the day was that the various cricket team members had the chance to show off their expertise in other aspects of their lives.

Although there were numerous other non-cricket people involved, such as fairground operators, and local councillors, most of the cricketers brought along their own interests and abilities to the proceedings.

Some of the players would contribute their day-to-day work experience. For instance Hypo would deal with all the fete's electrical requirements, and Trainset and Nutter would sort out the plumbing and drainage aspects for the day. Accountant Dave had a huge role, as he dealt with all of the financial side of the fete. But this at least meant that he could enjoy the day itself, whereas most of the others couldn't. The two salesmen, Bill and Des, were normally responsible for touting up trade from the customers. They would wander around the visiting throng, pointing them in the direction of this particular fair ride, or that particular sideshow, and selling raffle tickets as they did so.

Other team members would introduce their own hobbies to the proceedings. A good example of this was Architect Moaner, who had his own special collection of old American pinball machines. So, each year he hired a van, and brought part of his pride and joy along for viewing purposes. Similarly Mick was really into veteran traction engines, and, although he didn't own any himself, he had friends that did. So the cricket ground on Fete day had lots of mechanical equipment for the punters to admire.

It was very easy to find Omar an annual role at the Fete. Having been a Butlins Redcoat in his youth, he was excellent at all forms of entertainment. He would be linked up to the local radio, and have a roving commission of interviewing the customers, microphone in hand. He was very good at this, particularly with children. As well as his radio involvement, he would also be running the Punch and Judy Show.

Vic would spend most of his afternoon at the other end of the village, dealing with the Church-related functions, so he would not have any real involvement down at the ground. But it was expected that he would stroll along at some point, just to say hello, and to get a break away from his parishioners for a few minutes.

Because most of the plumbing work had been carried out before the day itself, Trainset was given the additional task of being the Chief Steward. The job was somewhat unspecific; he had been told to just keep on the move, and make sure that everything was operating correctly. He was to act as a sort of a non-policeman policeman.

Of the regular players, this just left Tantrum. He was more of a problem for the Cricket Club Fete Sub Committee. When he was with the team on normal summer Saturdays, he was very much 'cricket club orientated' in his attitude, particularly so since he had now begun his School Liaison Officer role. But Fete Saturday emphasised his divided loyalties. His yobbo mates would expect more from their leader than a toe-the-line approach; they would at least want to see him stir things up a bit. The cricket club were very much aware of all this, and so, rightly or wrongly, it was decided that Tantrum be left to do his own thing. He could help where he wanted to, but he wasn't given any specific task. However he was definitely expected to at least keep on the right side of the law, if nothing else.

The prime consideration of any local event like a village fete is usually that a date is chosen when the weather is most likely to remain friendly. And, as usual, the early September climate complied with expectations. It was beautifully warm and sunny. Vic and one of the Council members opened the fete at the church site, the message being relayed by tannoy down to the cricket ground. By this time there were several hundred in attendance at the cricket field. The fair rides were already doing well, and the gypsy with the crystal ball had a long queue outside her door. Trainset couldn't begin to understand the reason for eighty-five-year-old ladies wanting to have their futures predicted, but, as long as this unexplainable rationale was bringing a bit more dosh into the club, then he didn't really care. In the distance he could see Omar happily entertaining about a dozen five-year-olds. So far, everything was going very well.

Trainset was himself on the Fete Sub Committee, so he had to at least try to act responsibly, for a change. There was to be no acting the idiot today. He stood on Omar's rostrum to get a better vantage point, and he began his Chief Stewardship observations. Firstly, he looked around to see if both of the bars were now open, and functioning correctly. He was pleased to spot that the one nearest to Stalag 9 was already in operation and being run, apparently very efficiently, by one of the councillors and his wife. 'Good. There doesn't look like being any trouble down there today,' he whispered, thankfully.

The Fixture Secretary then turned his attentions towards the other bar. When he did so, he very nearly, to coin a well-worn phrase, produced kittens. He was all for a good laugh, particularly at the expense of others. But this was serious. Very, very, serious indeed. For some unaccountable reason, the second of the two Barmfield Cricket Club Beer Emporia Tents was currently being managed by a sixteen-year-old schoolboy. And, not only that, all of Tantrum's hard-case mates were hanging around as well, knocking back underage pints, no doubt having been charged next to nothing for them. How on earth Tantrum had managed to wheedle into that situation, Trainset could only guess. But what was more important than how he'd done it was how Trainset was going stop him doing it.

The Barmfield Number Two Batsman had to think on his feet. Making a big issue out of this, by bringing in some of the other players to help, might generate yet more problems. Too many cooks spoil the broth, and all that. It could end up being a repeat of the police versus the coalminers. But, at the same time, the Plumber daren't try to sort it out himself. He wasn't that manly. After all, the tearaways would then have only one bloke to beat up, rather than several. Over the course of the season, Tantrum had definitely changed his spots a bit. He was now much more grown up than he had been only a few months earlier. But he certainly wasn't the finished article yet, and Trainset was of the view that Tantrum's mates would still be more than capable of bringing out the worst in the schoolkid. The thing to do was to find someone who could sort Tantrum out better than Trainset could. The obvious first choice was Dave, because Tantrum had the greatest of respect for the ex-Skipper. But, if Dave couldn't be found, then Trainset needed to look for Tantrum's Dad. Or, as a last resort, a non-drinking version of one of the youngster's schoolmates.

The situation was now getting urgent. The real local constabulary, as opposed to Trainset's pretend version of one, would no doubt be making another courtesy call soon. But the Fixture Secretary hadn't seen Dave for an hour or two. Neither had he noticed Mr Tantrum Senior in the crowd. And there wasn't a surplus of Tantrum's non-boozing peers about, either, as most of the schoolboys were quaffing pints alongside their leader.

Trainset was the sort of guy who was more than happy letting others have all the responsibility, and then take great delight in criticising them for their efforts. He was an expert at finding fault in his team-mates. But he was not so good at doing important things off his own bat. He was beginning to get very worried.

He reached the talking to himself stage. 'Christ, we could get our ground closed for this. What the hell is Tantrum up to? Where the hell is Dave?' He started walking brusquely through the crowds, desperately seeking help.

He found Mick, but the senior bowler was preoccupied with showing off his traction engines to an admiring crowd. Moaner was similarly ensconced playing with one of his stupid waste of time pinball machines, and was currently surrounded by leather-clad motorcyclists. Trainset could disturb either of them, of course, but he would prefer to find help from someone who wasn't currently busy, because he knew that he'd only get slagged off later for upsetting some applecart or other. And, in any case, he couldn't see how Moaner or Mick could contribute any more than he could in trying to calm down a group of beer swilling troublemaking adolescents. His first priority was to find Dave. Then he could throw the problem in the direction of the ex-Skipper, and get back to his personal forte of pretending to be important.

By now Trainset was much nearer to the offending teenaged bar area. He could see the schoolboys, swilling ale as though there was no tomorrow. And he could also clearly see that Tantrum was the one providing the 'refreshments'. As sure as night follows day, there was no adult behind that bar counter. And, as sure as day follows night, there was also no way that the Chief Steward was going to wade into that shower of idiots, either. He'd get pummelled into kingdom come if he tried taking on that lot. Trainset moved swiftly up to level seven on his worry bead chart. 'Hell. What do I do? Shit, shit, shit.'

He began running, like a headless chicken, through the crowds. He had no idea where he was running to, or what he expected to achieve by doing it. The mixed up feelings in his brain reminded him of the afternoon twenty odd years before, when he'd got split up from his parents at the city fair. He'd panicked then, and he was panicking again now. He was sweating profusely, and his mind was in a complete whirl.

He saw Hypo in the pavilion. He was on his own. With a huge sigh of relief, Trainset raced towards him. The wicketkeeper had a piece of cable in one hand, and a huge bag of crisps in the other. He appeared to be busy sorting out a fusebox. He looked up to see his old school pal unlocking the door. Heavily out of breath, the Fixture Secretary gasped out his words.

'Hypo, I've got a real problem. Tantrum is serving behind the top bar. He's getting very drunk. And so are his mates. If the law turns up, we'll get clobbered. They'll shut the fete down, and if things go any more wrong, the cricket club will get shut down as well.'

Hypo wasn't much use. 'That's your job. You're the Steward. I've got to sort this lot out. Or there'll be no electricity, and that will also shut down the fete. Just get back up there and tell Tantrum & Co. to stop acting like idiots. You are twenty-seven years old, Trainset. Act like a man for a change. And, before you ask the next question, the answer is no. I've not seen Dave, or Tantrum's Dad, either. By the way, you don't know where the first aid box is, do you? I've got a bit of a headache.'

As the Plumber stroppily turned away, Hypo smirked at him. 'I think it's a case of 'Keep On Running', Trainset!'

Opening the pavilion door to leave, Trainset retorted to his tormentor. 'Thanks a bunch, Hypo. I love you, too. You fat babbling prat.'

The Barmfield Fete Cricket Club Sub-Committee Chief Steward did keep on running. He sprinted back through the throng, aggressively pushing bodies out of the way as he did so. This time he was much more focussed. He was going to sort out the little stupid boozer and his little stupid mates, even if he ended up in hospital by doing so. En route, he ran past PC Plod and WPC Ploddess. They must have recently arrived, and it wouldn't be long before they reached the same port of call as Trainset. The Number Two Batsman calculated that he had a couple of minutes, at most, to sort everything out. Otherwise, it would be curtains for the club, and the whole lot would be his fault.

Trainset made it to the Number Two Beer Emporium in record time. He threw himself at the group of youngsters, and he began knocking glasses out of their hands. There was lots of pushing and shoving. Drinks were flying in all directions. Two of the visiting teenaged lads were knocked onto the ground, one of them receiving a cut lip in the process. The Fixture Secretary Turned Raving Nutcase then grabbed hold of Tantrum and started to shake him, screaming wildly as he did so.

Tantrum stormed back at his attacker. 'You flaming idiot, Trainset. Those colas cost me about twenty quid. And you've broken about half a dozen glasses, as well. What the hell are you doing, you lunatic? Have you gone mad?'

As the facts began to slowly sink in, Mr Raving Nutcase stopped shaking the youngster. He also stopped screaming. His face changed from red to white. He stared sheepishly at the sixteen-year-old. 'Hell. Did you say cola, Tantrum? I thought you lot were drinking beer.'

'Of course we weren't drinking beer. You hare-brained effing plonker. I've brought my mates along, to try to get some of them interested in playing for the Club. And I've paid for several rounds of cola out of my own pocket. You've ruined the whole day. None of them will want to play for Barmfield now, will they?'

Trainset clutched at his only available straw. 'OK. Granted that you weren't drinking alcohol. But you still shouldn't have been serving behind that bar, should you?'

'I wasn't serving behind the bar. Dave was. He's still there now. I was just helping him by fetching the drinks from behind the counter, that's all. He must have been round the back, changing the beer pumps, when you came looking for him.'

Trainset peered into the Number Two Beer Emporium. There was Dave, serving pints to a couple of old guys. Having recently observed the fracas outside, the ex-Captain was giving Trainset a few funny looks as he did so. The Fixture Secretary stared back at Dave, everything now beginning to fall into place within his pathetic tiny little mind. He'd made a complete arsehole of himself. He'd been worrying stupid about nothing. Now he wanted to crawl into a hole, and never come out again.

But worse was yet to come for the depraved lunatic. The two police visitors had by now arrived at the scene of his crime.

Mr Plod tapped the Number Two Batsman on the shoulder. He started to speak. 'Getting a bit excited, are we, sir? Time for a bit of aggro, is it, sir? Felt like knocking seven bells out of these young lads, did we, sir? Had a few too many, have we, sir? Fancy a stroll down to the station with us, sir?'

Miss Ploddess took over. 'Hang on a minute Joe. Let's have a chat first'. She turned towards Trainset, and spoke very calmly, but with a slight smirk on her face.

'We witnessed most of the action as we walked up the hill. It was quite good, about seven out of ten, I reckon. I'm not sure whether you'll quite make World Heavyweight Champion, because you're a bit too puny. But your right hook's not bad. We'll probably arrest you in a minute or two, sir, but let's hear the other side of the story first. It's down to these young lads to decide whether they want to press charges. And, if they choose to have you charged, we'll then need statements from everybody. If I were one of these very well behaved youngsters, I'd definitely have you taken in, but it's up to them, sir. While they are thinking about what decision to make, let's start with your name and address, shall we, sir? And no wisecracks, please, sir. We've heard them all before, so nothing is funny any more. We'll have your proper name and address. Not Cassius Clay, or Miss Tinkerbell, thank you.'

The young lads didn't press charges. Tantrum and his mates explained fully and honestly what had happened, and how Trainset had, not for the first time, got the wrong end of the stick. The lad with the cut lip helped further, by saying that he'd caused the damage with his new razor, at home, earlier in the day. Dave also backed up the teenagers' story, and the Fixture Secretary was eventually let off with a caution.

The fete was a great success for the cricket club, for the church, and for the village of Barmfield in general. Bill and Des had sold countless raffle tickets, and Omar had been brilliant in his Chief Entertainer role. But Trainset wasn't too bothered about such trifles. He was exhausted, he'd almost been arrested, he'd upset Tantrum and Dave, he'd put off numerous potential young cricketers from joining the Club, and he'd made himself a complete laughing stock. He was so embarrassed about the day's happenings that he'd not risked attending one of the bars to drown his sorrows. He was acutely aware that he was never going to be allowed to live down that September day. Never. He would be stuck with it for years to come.

Twenty-four hours earlier, the Barmfield Fixture Secretary had been eagerly looking forward to the following week's final match, but now he wasn't looking forward to the damned thing at all. He wished that the season had already finished. He drove sulkily home, his stupid tail very much between his stupid legs.

Steve was nearly there. He just had a couple more chapters to write. He started on the one about the last game of the season...

CHAPTER EIGHTEEN
MATCH 16

THE LAST TIME

It was the grand finale of the season. Barmfield were at Battenborough. It was a typical late summer's day, with a hazy sun starting to force its way through the misty atmosphere. It was feeling much cooler now; gone were those balmy summer afternoons of Brindon and Allesbush.

Battenborough was only about three miles from Barmfield. Other than Wollatown, it was the nearest away fixture. Moaner lived in the village, but had chosen to play for Barmfield a few years ago, presumably because the Battenborough lads all hated him even more than the Barmfield blokes did. It was an attractive little place, with several large old properties, and Moaner lived in one of these. The village also had a nature reserve, and was in a pleasant situation adjacent to the river. The ground sat in a central position, near to the pub. As he arrived, Trainset had a job finding a space, as the car park was already virtually full.

Various players had a bit of a go at the now very sheepish Trainset, about events of the previous Saturday. But, luckily, Bill was without his postiche, and this helped to deflect the line of attack away from the Plumber. Bill's bald cranium was distinctly lighter in colour than it had been pre-wig; in fact it was as white as snow. This was presumably because Mr Ruggie had, more often than not, protected it from the ravages of the English Summer. The Captain's overall appearance reminded Trainset of a Christmas tree, with a white fairy on top. But on a day like today such a thought was best kept under wraps, especially taking into account the Plumber's own embarrassing problems at the fete. So, unusually for him, he kept his mouth shut.

Why Bill was not wigged up was a source of several questions. But the answer to this conundrum soon arrived. In response to some of the less derogatory banter about his head, Bill spoke positively. 'I've decided that I don't need a toupee. Rather more to the point, I don't need the verbals that come with it. I've chucked the thing in the bin. We are going to win the title today, and I'm not wearing a ruddy syrup on the presentation photographs.' The others cheered loudly.

There was another pre-match surprise. 'Can you all shut up a minute' said Moaner, 'I'd just like to announce that I'm packing up after today. Bill thought it best if I mentioned it before the match. I know that you all hate me, but I still want to help you win this one. It would be good to finish my career with a League title. So this is the last time for me.'

It was difficult for the others to avoid repeating their previous raucous shouts of approval. Trainset in particular saw this as another opportunity to change the line of fire from being aimed at him. 'Sorry about that, Moaner,' he said, trying to hold his glee in check. Further support came from Omar. 'We'll miss you. Moaner,' lied the Number Three, rather blatantly.

Bill spoke again. 'Yes. Sorry that you're finishing, Moaner. But, as it happens, you are not the only one.

Unfortunately it's not Trainset who's leaving us. It's Des. He has just had a word with me. It'll be his last match today as well. So let's win it for these two, please, lads.'

Whilst Bill was on the subject of retirements, Trainset remembered what Vic had said earlier in the Summer. He turned towards the Number Five, and asked the question that was probably on the mind of several of the team. 'What about you, Vic? Are you really going to pack it in this year, as well? You said that you would, earlier in the season.'

Vic responded to the contrary. 'No. Bill's asked me to carry on. I might have a bit of help at the church next summer, so I'm hoping that my timekeeping will be better. Therefore I'm going to play again. Assuming that's OK with you lot, of course. I know that you're all still annoyed with me. I've felt guilty all season. I don't suppose that I've got many friends here now. In fact I feel a bit like Moaner Mark Two. But I'd like to try to make things up to you all, next year. So I'm giving it another go. By the way, Trainset, I hear that you made yourself look somewhat stupid last weekend. In fact, you made yourself look very stupid indeed. Have you got a criminal record now? And have you apologised to young Mr Tantrum?'

Apart from Moaner and Trainset, everyone was pleased with Vic's response. But the announcement of two retirees was still a bombshell. Trainset could see why Bill had made sure that the news was announced before the match, rather than afterwards. Moaner had spent years upsetting people, and so his departure was like a breath of fresh air to the rest of the team. The situation with Des was a bit different. Some of the players liked him, some didn't. But they all had a great respect for him, and so would no doubt be trying their hardest today to send him out on a high note. And the fact that Vic was still a Barmfield bloke meant that there was a chance that the wounds would eventually heal between the Vicar and the rest of them. The other eight players felt even more determined now. The pre-match news was a masterstroke by Bill, in the opinion of the Barmfield Fixture Secretary.

They took to the field. This was it, the culmination of all of their hopes and dreams. One more victory, and they'd be Champions. A sprinkling of the spectators applauded their arrival on to the outfield; this had never happened before in Trainset's experience of playing club cricket. The hubbub led him to survey the large crowd in more detail.

He spotted a brown haired girl, sitting in a deckchair behind the boundary rope at long off. 'Christ,' he enthused 'That's Sue Taylor.' She was about a hundred yards away, but he was still sure that it was his ex. He couldn't make out whether she was waving to him, or wafting away a late summer wasp. So he thought better of waving back, just in case.

Sexy Sam and Janet were also on the boundary edge, talking to a couple of the opposition tea ladies. It would be a big day for Janet today, with Biased Bob umpiring for the last time. She had sensed that she might be the centre of attention, and had clearly made a big effort to look the part, sporting not only a new hairdo, but also a recently purchased dark grey trouser suit. Sexy Sam also looked good, as usual, in her tight jeans and polo necked sweater.

Trainset then witnessed a sight to behold. Mick's grandchildren, Jake and Katie, were also in attendance. But, much more significantly, their Mum and Dad were also there. Incredibly the four of them appeared to be a proper family, at last. Mum was holding Katie's hand, and Dad was having catching practice with Jake, using a tennis ball. 'I don't believe it. Those brainless parents are showing some interest in their kids,' the Plumber mused. 'Mick will be chuffed to death.' Trainset had never met Mick's son in law before, but he immediately looked to be quite a sporty sort of bloke. He recalled that Mick had once mentioned that he was a very good golfer, playing off a mere two-stroke handicap. The Plumber wondered if he might prove to be a good cricketer as well. Perhaps the new Des?

It got even better. Many of the wives had turned up. Hiding their respective husband's animosities from each other, Mrs June Price, Mrs Rose Wickham, Mrs Joan Fork, and Mrs Anne Whiteside were all happily chatting. And the heavily pregnant Alice Maughan was also settling herself into a deckchair, alongside Vic's young sons.

But the greatest sight of all was that of Omar's Mum. Trainset had met her several times before, when picking Omar up at his home for midweek boozing evenings. This was before Persil's arrival on the scene, of course. Mrs Singh Senior must have had Omar late in life, because she looked about 70, and her son was only 24. She couldn't speak a word of English, and the Number Two Batsman knew that her confidence level outside her flat, in her now adopted big foreign city, was very low. So to see her make the effort to witness Omar play cricket struck Trainset as a big thing for her to do. He was impressed that she had shown such a supportive attitude. She looked resplendent in a bright pink sari, so there wasn't much chance of anyone missing the fact that she was there.

He saw Omar run across to her, and introduce her to some of the other female attendees. Omar physically moved Mrs Singh next to them, so that she could have someone to listen to. Although she would have no idea what they were talking about, it was still preferable to sitting on her own. There was no sign of Persil, so no potentially embarrassing Mum versus Wife situations were likely to take place today.

Trainset moved to his position at slip, and his mind returned to the events on the field. He surveyed their three retirees.

Firstly he saw Moaner taking his position, a few yards away, in the gulley. Although Trainset hated the stupid old fart, he was still very much aware that this was a big day in Moaner's life, perhaps the biggest. He looked fidgety and ill at ease. And he appeared suddenly much older than his 47 years, his ashen face seemingly attempting to match his greying hair. The occasion must have got to him, possibly for the first time in 30 odd years of playing cricket. He was pacing around all over the place, occasionally performing minor stretching exercises as he did so. He also appeared to be verbally geeing himself up.

Then there was Des, Trainset's opening partner for the

past four years. He'd scored his century now, so he'd achieved his lifelong ambition. But a win today would be the icing on the cake for him. He looked much happier than Moaner. He was at the bowler's end, standing alongside Bill, presumably discussing fielding positions with the Skipper, and the two of them were laughing and joking as though it was a pub match.

'Funny how nerves affect people differently,' the Fixture Secretary mused.

Finally there was Biased Bob. He was behind the bowler's stumps, ready for the off. He'd got one of the bails in his hand, and was making some sort of scratch mark on the ground with it. While Trainset watched, he saw Nutter walk up, and take a shiny new ball from Biased Bob's hand. The umpire took Nutter's sweater in return. It struck Trainset that holding Nutter's sweater all afternoon might not be the most pleasant of tasks. Fast bowlers usually sweat a lot. Add that to Nutter being in the sewage business, and it all must have meant more than an occasional whiff for poor old Biased Bob. 'Perhaps that's the reason for his poor umpiring performances.' Trainset subtly smirked. 'He's probably been suffering from the effects of some sort of gas attack every Saturday afternoon.' Then reality hit him; he thought about Biased Bob's serious eye illness, and about the fact that he would never be standing there again. The Fixture Secretary stopped chuckling.

Bill wandered down to join the behind-the-wicket fielders. It was time to start. With the emotions of the sideshow distractions, Trainset had a tear in his eye as Nutter began to charge in.

Nutter's first over was somewhat wild. So it was eight for no wicket when Omar started his spell from the other end. However, it didn't take Trainset's best mate long to make the breakthrough. His fourth ball was a fast away swinger, which led to a fine catch by Hypo, diving away in front of Trainset at first slip. There was a trickle of applause from their vast away support. Ten for one after two overs.

The Battenborough innings followed the route of a typical

local cricket match. There was a good stand here and there, but wickets also fell regularly. Again, Dave bowled well, picking up nine, ten and jack in the process. So it was 186 all out, and the players went off for tea.

Unlike the other 22 participants, Omar and Trainset didn't go straight to the pavilion. They did a quick tour of the boundary, thanking their supporters for their attendance. They concentrated their efforts on Sue and Mrs Singh. Sue told her ex-boyfriend that she still wasn't sure about her future with a cricketer, but that she wouldn't miss this match 'For all the tea in China'. By the time Trainset got to the food, most of it had gone, and Bill was already moaning at him to get his pads on. So he just managed a quick cuppa and a piece of carrot cake, before being manhandled by his Captain towards the changing room. Des was already in there, applying several layers of protection to every conceivable body part.

The Fixture Secretary spoke first. 'Good luck, Des. Both for today, and for the future. We'll miss you, Des.'

'Thanks, Trainset. I'll miss you lot as well. But I'd promised June that if I ever got a century, then I'd pack it in and spend more time with her. So that's what I'm going to do from now on. We might even move house. June likes the countryside, and I can work as a rep from there just as easily. You can have some of my bats and pads and things after today, if you want them, Trainset. As long as you don't use the bats to attack Tantrum or the police, of course.'

They went out to bat. This time it was not only Trainset who had moist eyes.

Neither Des nor Trainset did very well. Both of them just scraped into double figures. The ball was seaming around a lot, due to the humid conditions. Most of the other recognised batsmen fared equally badly. Getting 187 was becoming a tall order. They struggled to 91 for 6, and things were looking bleak. Dave was still there, and Hypo was now on his way out to join him. The Barmfield lads knew that it was possible that they could still be champions, whether or not they lost this match. But it was unlikely that all the other results would go their way. And, in any case, they desperately wanted to win the League by themselves, rather than being handed it on a plate by one of the other clubs.

It was by now becoming a very tense affair. By the time that Hypo reached the crease, the crowd had gone quiet. The Battenborough lads could still finish second themselves; so taking advantage of Barmfield's nervous stuttering was very much in their interests.

Dave and Hypo took the score past the psychological three-figure barrier. But it was slow going. They needed to speed things up, otherwise there would not be sufficient overs left. With the score on 111, Hypo took a risk going a quick single. But his sheer size let him down, and he was run out by a good three yards.

So 76 runs were still needed, with three wickets left, when Bill strode out to join Dave. It was the League's worst batsman on his way to the crease, so Barmfield had, in effect, only two wickets left. Or that's what they all thought.

They were proved wrong. Bill came good, at last. He'd played 15 matches, and never looked like scoring a proper run. He'd been bowled all over the place several times, and on the few occasions that he'd actually made contact with the ball, he'd only succeeded in hitting it straight into a fielder's hands, or onto his stumps. He'd got so many Achilles heels that he needed specially made socks. And yet here, in the biggest game of the lot, he started to bat well. He even hit a couple of fours. It seemed unbelievable to the others, but before their very eyes it was happening. With Dave, as usual, batting superbly, and guiding him along, Bill batted to the end. Dave finished on 75 not out, Bill on 32 not out. Barmfield had won with an over to spare.

As the spectators thronged around the pavilion, Dave characteristically condescended to let Bill lead the players from the field. The Skipper was mobbed by all and sundry. This was the perfect end to the perfect season. Barmfield were League champions, and Bill had been their inspiration. Closely followed by the ever-reliable Dave, of course. Trainset wasn't sure that a celebratory lap around the boundary was quite the done thing for a local cricket team, but Tantrum led them all on one, anyway. The Fixture Secretary felt that the honour of leading the celebrations should really have belonged to Dave or Bill, rather than Tantrum, but this was not the right time to start an argument with their sixteen-year-old hard case. So they all followed him around the field, waving and shouting as they went.

To round things off nicely, Biased Bob hadn't given one bad decision all afternoon. As he reluctantly ambled off behind the players, several of them shook his hand and wished him well. Biased Bob had spent the most enjoyable days of his life with Barmfield CC. His eyes were streaming with tears as he trudged into a cricket pavilion for the last time.

Everyone had a great time afterwards. The Battenborough bar took a real hammering; even Mrs Singh was spotted downing a sherry or two. Moaner and Des both made little goodbye speeches. Biased Bob was invited to do likewise, but his still-streaming eyes prevented him from doing so, and Janet carried out the task on his behalf. Trainset had expected Sue to run away immediately after the match, but she didn't; she was by his side, fully joining in as though she was one of the team. Things were looking good again in that respect. Bill was interviewed, on the pub phone, by the local radio. Vic spent the whole evening thanking everyone for putting up with his timekeeping problems, Hypo failed to mention any current illness or injury, and Dave was again voted player of the year. Omar and Trainset laughed and laughed all night. It was midnight before most of them left.

What a day! What a season!

Steve Smith was ecstatic. It had all gone really well. His stupid employer couldn't fail to be impressed. And the whole thing had only taken him about ten weeks. So he was only about a fortnight late. The Plumber began typing his last chapter...

CHAPTER NINETEEN
THE END OF SEASON
FUNCTION

SATURDAY NIGHT'S ALRIGHT FOR FIGHTING

We now move on to a Saturday evening in November, about ten weeks after the final match. It was the annual Dinner and Dance, which always took place at a posh hotel in the local city. The Barmfield players were virtually all in attendance. In order to boost the numbers, several of them had, as usual, invited outside guests. This year there were four tables, each one comprising eight people.

Trainset had now regained Sue as his regular girlfriend, and they were sitting on Table Number Three with Biased Bob, Janet, and a couple of Biased Bob's neighbours. Also with them were Nutter and Tantrum, neither of whom had brought partners.

On Table Number Two were Dave, Sexy Sam, Mick and Joan Fork, Tim, Blondie and two of Blondie's female teenaged friends. Both of the girls were similar in character and dress sense to Blondie herself. But were yet more tarty, if that was possible. For the purpose of this summary of events, they will be referred to as Scrubbette A and Scrubbette B.

Table Number One comprised Vic and Alice Maughan, Moaner and Rose Wickham, Hypo and Mrs Cudleigh, Omar, and one of Omar's male Indian relatives. Omar had been unable to persuade Mrs Singh to turn up, and he'd not risked asking Persil. Hypo's wife was not a regular attendee at matches, so most of the others didn't really know her very well.

Des and June Price were sitting at Table Number Four, along with Bill and Anne Whiteside, Bill's mother in law and her 'boyfriend,' and the two guest speakers. One of the speakers was Fred O'Connor, the local mayor. The other was Brian Routledge, a well-known professional cricketer.

There were pre-dinner drinks in the foyer, and the attendees took their places at their respective tables. Everyone was looking good, the women in their finery, and the blokes in their DJ's. Omar was the exception to the rule. He looked a bit of a dipstick, a Scottish kilt and pink brothel creepers seeming somewhat inappropriate for a Kenyan Indian at a rather upmarket English function. But apparently he'd left his proper dinner trousers and his shoes at his uncle's chip shop in Manchester, for some inexplicable reason. Luckily Bill had brought several spare dinner jackets, 'Just in case', so at least Omar looked relatively sane from the waist up.

Vic was invited to say grace, and everyone started on the soup. So far so good.

Unfortunately it was around this point that things began to go somewhat haywire. Trainset witnessed many of the happenings with his own eyes, others he didn't. This is a summary based on what he saw, and on other people's later accounts of events.

The problems began on Table Four. The 'boyfriend,' who must have been 75 if he was a day, had apparently been drinking rather heavily before the meal. So, in his hazy state, he somehow managed to get his soup bowl and his serviette intertwined, and half a pint of borsch ended up in the lap of Fred O'Connor. This was bad enough in itself, but Fred's political bent was slightly further to the right than that of Hitler. Had the soup been cream of tomato, the boyfriend would doubtless have got away with it. But being anywhere near Communist produce appeared to have more of an effect on his temper than the fact that his crotch was totally drenched in beetroot.

Grimacing with pain, Fred shouted out. 'I thought that this left wing rubbish was supposed to be served cold.' On his way to the loo, he could be seen applying ice and napkins to his private parts.

While Fred was sorting himself out, there was another drink-fuelled event on Table Two. Scrubbette B, in response to a perfectly reasonable comment about her under age drinking habits from Joan Fork, had suggested to Mick's inquisitive wife that she should 'Fork off back to her forking coven.' This led to a bit of a fracas, which only cooled when Mick secretly bribed one of the young male waiters to offer the rather unpleasant young lady a lift home at the end of the evening. Mick had made sure that he had picked one of the more masculine looking ones, which hadn't been easy.

This was a masterstroke from Mick, and Table Two could relax again for a while. But, unfortunately, it didn't stop problems occurring elsewhere. Tantrum threw a friendly bread roll at Nutter, missed, and hit Mrs Neighbour in the eye. Janet took her to Reception for ice pack treatment.

Table Two was again brought to the fore, when Scrubbette A became involved in some sort of altercation with Sexy Sam, over the teenager's rather blatant attempts to throw herself all over Dave.

However the worst problem of all occurred on Table One. Somehow, Persil had found out about the event, and had by now turned up, with the intention of giving Omar an earbashing for not inviting her to attend. But she had not arrived without preparation. Firstly she was dressed to the nines, and secondly she had clearly imbibed a few glasses of throat-clearing linctus. She was not only very loud, but also very drunk. She commenced proceedings, by hurling insults at all and sundry. In an attempt to keep the screaming imbecilic bitch away from the rest of the diners, Omar dragged Persil outside. But she was on such fine form that the Car Park still felt like an extension to the Dining Room, all of the guests clearly hearing her raving tirade from their seats.

By the time that the meal was completed, and the speakers were ready to start, some sort of order had just about been restored. Fred got up to speak. He was standing next to his seat, as it had been earlier decided that using the stage for speeches was a bit OTT for such a small gathering.

'On behalf of the Council, I'd like to congratulate. Oh, shit.....'

The reason for his decision to stop speaking soon became apparent. Boyfriend was at it again. He'd been to the bar, and he'd not quite been able to regain his seat before the Mayor stood up. The old codger was therefore in a desperate rush to get back to his own position, in a rather hopeless attempt to avoid causing any further embarrassment. Unfortunately his haste had entirely the opposite effect. Pints of beer rained in on Mr O'Connor, seemingly from all angles. Boyfriend collapsed on the carpet, and, for completely different reasons, Trainset and several of the others did likewise. It was absolutely hilarious. The Fixture Secretary's stomach ached so much, that it reminded him of the day when Bill first turned up in his wig.

Mr Mayor again retired to the loo, whimpering as he went. He was heard to say something along the lines of 'If I receive one more attack, I'm going to thump somebody. And then I'm calling the police.'

Trainset waved across at Omar. Now was the ideal time for their carefully rehearsed routine. The band had been pre-warned, and was ready to play. Most of the other team members joined Trainset and Omar on stage, for a hilarious send-up of Skipper Bill. Wearing long wigs, and carrying children's plastic cricket bats, they sang a rousing rendition of 'Bill Whiteside Won't You Please Come Home.' This was then followed by an old 'Reparata and the Delrons' number, entitled 'Captain Of Your Ship.' Other than Bill, the spectators clearly loved the performance. Blondie and the Scrubbettes were seen to be heartily singing along, whilst exposing their knickers to all and sundry. The entertainers re-took their seats to a standing ovation from all except one.

Bill needed to halt the downhill spiral of events. And to do so rapidly. He asked Brian Routledge to take over proceedings. The Skipper's idea here was clearly to quickly get everyone's mind off Mayors and hairpieces, before the whole evening degenerated into complete farce. As it turned out, such a decision was unfortunately about half an hour too late.

Mr Routledge was shaking with laughter, and even starting his own address was difficult for him. He mumbled a few words, giggled, waffled something that made no sense at all, and then coughed. He tried to start again, but failed. It was all getting a bit much for the poor bloke.

Bill took the bull by the horns. He hurried over and intervened, announcing yet another change in plan. 'The speeches will come later. Let's start the dancing.' Brian sat down in hysterics. He'd probably missed out on a large fee, but the comedy value had been much greater.

Luckily the band members hadn't all dispersed to the bar, and so they were still raring to go. That's perhaps a slight exaggeration, in that the trombonist was by now virtually legless, and the drummer had nipped outside for a fag. But, within a couple of minutes, music restarted and sanity was temporarily restored.

Trainset smooched away with Sue. Whilst doing so, they watched other couples come and go. They smiled at some of the embarrassingly underwhelming attempts at tripping the light fantastic. Most of the participants hadn't got a clue. How one couple could be performing a waltz while another was doing the chicken dance to exactly the same tune, was something of a mystery. The Plumber and his girlfriend quietly discussed the possibility of the next year's function being in fancy dress. They couldn't stop giggling at some of the possibilities that such an event might throw up. But the two renewed lovers were more eagerly anticipating the next major incident of the current evening, rather than the one 52 weeks away. Ideally they wanted another 'Boyfriend Related' incident to occur. They didn't have to wait long.

The third number started. Rather appropriately, it was the band's own version of 'Saturday Night's Alright For Fighting.' Trainset and Sue saw Bill's mother in law, complete with Boyfriend, join in the proceedings. 'This should be good,' said Sue.

It was good. Boyfriend was struggling to stand, never mind dance. This was partly due to his age, partly due to his alcohol intake. He began to slip, and in trying to prevent a full collapse, grabbed at the nearest person for support. It was just his bad luck that, at that precise moment, the Mayor happened to be passing by, on his way back from the Toilet.

The rest, as they say, is history.

EPILOGUE

Steve Smith sat down across the table from Ted Carruthers. They were back in the posh office this time, presumably because the secretive element of the Plumber's undercover work was now about to be made public. The host was wearing his normal pinstripe outfit, whereas the ex-Barmfield Fixture Secretary was, as usual, in his plumbing gear, the stuff that he wore all day every day. The visitor hadn't had a bath or shower for a week, but he'd still not clocked on why the Deputy Editor again appeared to be unduly over-interested in maintaining high volumes of airflow through fully open windows. Despite a mid winter howling gale blowing outside. In the eyes of Steve Smith, the reason for such activity was to temporarily prevent internal secretarial staff from applying their ears to the keyhole. At least for the next few minutes, anyway. His new mate Ted was clearly damping down the conversation by incorporating external traffic and wind noise. There was no coffee and no biscuits.

The big newspaperman started first.

'Thanks for coming in again, Steve. And thanks for what

you've done. I've read it through a couple of times, and so has my Sports Editor. We both think that it's very good. It ties in well with some of our own newspaper articles. And also with some rather more lurid reports, which were printed in the other local newspaper at the time. That paper was called 'The Echo'. I don't know if you remember it Steve? It's not in existence now, of course. Anyway, I've found a particularly good old edition of The Echo here, which reports on your end of season function. There are several pages about the evening. The front-page headline reads 'Lord Mayor Quits His Position.' Below this were various sub-sections, with headings such as 'Underage Call Girls Involved,' 'Local Businesswoman Charged With Racial Abuse,' 'Old Lady Attacked With Bread Roll,' 'County Cricket League Kicks Out Barmfield,' etc., etc. It must have been quite a good night?'

Steve Smith responded. 'The evening itself was brilliant. Omar, Sue and I laughed and laughed for weeks afterwards. But, being truthful, we weren't so happy with those Echo reports. In fact, most of us were a bit aggrieved about them. We felt that The Bloody Echo had completely taken the gloss off what we'd achieved. After all, we had won the Division, you know. There didn't seem to be much in their articles about that. It was much more about the things that we'd done wrong, as opposed to those that we'd done right. Afterwards most of us blamed that so-called newspaper for getting us chucked out of the League. It was the beginning of the end for Barmfield, that was. And don't forget that Tantrum and Young Tim went on to play County Cricket; in fact Young Tim was a hair's breadth away from playing for England. So, in retrospect, The Effing Echo did us no favours. No favours at all.'

The Deputy Editor continued. 'I realise that now, Steve. I was only in a junior position at that time, of course. But I have to admit that I was at The Echo. And that I wrote a lot of the stuff myself. In fact, reporting on your demise helped me begin my inexorable rise up the greasy newspaper pole. As I said a few weeks ago, sensationalism sells newspapers, I'm afraid. Particularly sex. But, before you thump me, please let me carry on.'

Steve Smith's face turned white with anger, and he started to get out of his chair. He clenched his fists, and he stared at the host with absolute hatred in his eyes. But he had insufficient time to say or do anything, before the lookalike Russian Dictator started again.

'Calm down a minute, Steve, and listen to me. Off the record, I've known for twenty-five years that what I did to Barmfield Cricket Club was not very clever. My reports were completely OTT. I know that now. At the time, I just wanted to make myself a bit of a hero. And I was ambitious. But, for the last ten years or so, the events of the past have been gnawing at me, particularly as my grandfather used to be an opening batsman for Barmfield. You didn't know that, did you? He was matey with Biased Bob Jones. Anyway, after a while I felt that I just had to do something about it. Of course, I cannot change history, and so I can't recreate Barmfield Cricket Club. But I can do other things, in order to 'put the record straight' a bit. And that's what the next fifteen or twenty weeks will aim to do. Please keep all this to yourself, Steve.'

Steve Smith responded. 'Well, that's a turn up for the books. You're now telling me that this whole writing palaver has been, hitting the nail on the head, just a way of exorcising your personal guilt trip. You didn't stick a pin into Barmfield CC, did you? I wasn't picked at random, was I? Christ, this is a real thunderbolt, this is. I feel like smacking you in the teeth. Not for the first time, I might add.'

The Plumber didn't smack the Sub Editor in the teeth. Instead, they stared at each other for a minute or two, pondering events. Steve thought deeply, before carrying on.

'You know, I loved my cricket at Barmfield, particularly that season. I didn't realise how much I miss the game nowadays, until I started writing this article for you. Cricket used to help me to laugh a lot, but nowadays I'm just a boring moaning old fart. I wish that I were playing again now. I think that Danton Over Stale may still be in existence, so I might give them a call in the Spring. Depending on what Wendy says, of course. Knowing her, there's bound to be some major problem with it.'

The ex-Fixture Secretary kept going. 'Mr Carruthers, not only have you done yourself a favour, but you've done me one as well. So I'm not going to try to thump you. In any case, you're much bigger than me, so you'd most likely flatten me with your first punch. Also, if I did flukily manage to smack you one first, there'd be another cricketer headline article in tomorrow night's edition, wouldn't there?'

The now remorseful Sub Editor smiled, before responding. 'Well, I hope Danton Over Stale works out, if that's what you want to do. Anyway, thanks again, Steve. As I said, we are really pleased with your article. We'll have to tone some of it down a bit, because many of our readers are only youngsters. But, in essence, we want to keep the same general format. I know that we agreed a fee a couple of months ago, but I'd like to give you a bit of a bonus, as well, if that's OK?'

Steve Smith tried to appear nonchalant. As usual he failed. His answer didn't hide his pride. 'Whatever. It's up to you. I'm not destitute, you know.'

'I'll add another thousand on, out of my own pocket. Hopefully that's sorted it all out OK? But, whilst you're here, Steve, there are a couple of other things. The first one is that we think that what you've written might well be very suitable as a comedy series on TV. I know several BBC and ITV people who might well be interested. I could give them a call if you wish? The other point is that we understand that you used to play soccer. How about doing the same thing again about your old football club? Fancy a coffee and some biscuits, Steve, while you think about it?'

Mr Pinstripe picked up the phone, and ordered refreshments. He then left the room, in order that his visitor could privately consider the situation.

Steve Smith's mind was in overdrive, as he contemplated his future as a best-selling author. 'TV? Football? Fame? Fortune? Christ, that old scorebook was worth keeping, after all. Now, what can I remember about Barmfield Football Club? Well, Teflon Turner was definitely the goalie. He was called that because he could never get the ball to stick to his hands. Then I reckon that we had a bloke called Bill Bates. Or was it Bob Bates? Anyway, Batesy played at the back. He was a butcher, in all senses of the word. He got sent off every other week. The left-winger was definitely Freddie The Frog; he was a good mate of mine. For some reason unbeknown to the rest of the lads, Freddie had developed a heavy Brummie accent, despite being conceived during a holiday in Jersey. To Freddie the Frog, the ball was generally irrelevant. He spent most of the game posing on the touchline, homing in on female spectators between the ages of three and eighty-five. I can also vaguely recall a Norwegian full back, who played every game in his own little world, because he never understood a ruddy thing that anybody said to him. There was one match when, after half time, he mistakenly started playing for the opposition. And the team manager, coach, and groundsman was a chap called Stuttering Stan. He was a character as well. Referees often had to curtail his half time team talks, either to prevent darkness falling, or to stop rigor mortis setting in. Yes, this is great. It's all coming back to me now. There must be another good book on its way with that lot.'

Steve's mind went back to cricket. 'There could be spin-off's from the cricket club stories, as well. For instance, a TV series about Blondie and the Scrubbettes, and another about the Vicar of Barmfield. Yes, this is brilliant, this is.'

Steve's reminiscences were abruptly curtailed. The host had returned. The Deputy Editor sat down and spoke. 'What do you reckon, then, Steve?'

'Well. You've got to remember that I'm still doing my Plumbing. The business has suffered a lot already. So I'll need more dosh if I try to do any more writing for you. Other than that, I'm interested.'

'Good', said the Deputy Editor. 'Shall we say £20K for the football stories? As regards the TV side of things, I'll have to come back to you on that. But it's looking good.'

On the drive home, Steve chatted away to the steering wheel. He'd made a success of his life, at last. He was looking forward to telling his wife about it all. 'Wait until The Missus hears about this one. £20,000 for a week or two's writing. Wow! And then there's the probability of TV performances, as well. This is what I've really needed for a long while. It's given me a kick-start. My confidence is coming back. It's brilliant, this is. And I'm sure all this will help my relationship with Wendy. In fact, I'm going to take her out for a meal to celebrate. She'll like that. It's a while since we've been anywhere together. I might even tell her that I love her, if I can pluck up the courage. Then we could plan a nice holiday. This will be a completely new beginning for us, this will.'

He turned on the CD player, and he began to sing along to the 1960's music. 'Come all without, come all within, you ain't seen nothing like the mighty Steve' was followed by 'Those were the days, my friend, I thought they'd never end, I loved my cricket and I loved my wife.' Finally, as he turned into his drive, he was well into 'Dedicated follower of Barmfield'.

He got out of his van, grabbed his important papers, and opened the front door. He couldn't wait to tell Wendy about newspapers, and books, and cricket, and so on.

There was a note on the mat. He picked it up. He began to read.

'Dear Steve. I can't stand things anymore. When we first met, you were sporty and popular. We went out a lot, and we had loads of friends. I really enjoyed it when you played cricket and football. But we never do anything together these days. We never go to the cinema, or eat out, do we? I wouldn't have minded if you'd started playing cricket again; I'd sooner you did that than just sit on the sofa with your TV and your beer. And why don't you use your brain occasionally? You're a bright bloke, but you don't seem the slightest bit interested in things like newspapers or books. And you don't seem to want to earn any proper money, either. I've left you, and I'm not telling you where I've gone. There isn't anyone else involved. But I've just had enough of it all. I'll miss you, Steve. Look after yourself. Goodbye.'

Steve Smith fetched a can of lager from the fridge. He turned on the Lounge TV, and he sat down on the settee. He flicked through the channels, and found a football match. It was Liverpool, playing against a virtually unknown foreign side.

Steve had a very uncomfortable feeling that he'd been there somewhere before.

Then the phone rang ......

*   *   *   *   *

About the Author

John Meller was born in Nottingham in 1950. Having passed his 11 plus, he moved on to a local Grammar school, where he achieved a modicum of educational success. In 1968 he was accepted by the local Regional College of Technology (now Nottingham Trent University), on a four year Quantity Surveying degree sandwich course. He obtained his BSc in 1972, and then joined the local office of a national quantity surveying practice. He achieved RICS qualification in 1973. In later years he set up his own Project Management and Quantity Surveying business, which in 2013 is still going strong despite John's personal retirement in 2000. Nowadays John occasionally carries out property development tasks, by purchasing and upgrading domestic properties for sale or rent.

John met Judith in 1981, and they married two years later. Judith went on to become headteacher of a local Infant and Nursery school. They now live in Kegworth, adjacent to East Midlands airport. They have no children.

During his school and business life, John began to take an active interest in many local sports. He became a county-standard hockey player, and a regular golfer. But his greatest love has always been cricket, and he has played for many years, albeit at a very average standard. At 62 he still turns out occasionally for a local club. John has also played social-level soccer, squash and tennis. His support for Nottingham Forest Football Club and Nottinghamshire County Cricket Club is lifelong.

John's other interests include writing, trains, gardening, foreign holidays, and DIY.

Printed in Great Britain
by Amazon